What *Romantic Times* says about Harlequin Temptation and Tiffany White:

"…an erotic romp filled with seductive sensuality."

—LOVE, ME

"Tiffany White uses her writing expertise to bring us an outrageously delightful heroine with a sinfully active imagination."

—NAUGHTY TALK

"…FORBIDDEN FANTASY [is] a magnificent example of Harlequin Temptation at its very best.… What follows is a lush, exotic blend of sensual fantasy and marital insight."

—FORBIDDEN FANTASY

When asked to describe her life, **Tiffany White** told us that in her fantasies she flies to the coast for weekend visits with friends, sees all the latest movies, fills her closets with the latest fashions and regularly wins the *Romantic Times* Most Sensual Author award. In reality, Tiffany has gone to her office dressed in sweatshirts and leggings, has written four books in the past year, goes home to veg out with videos and has become the Susan Lucci of the coveted *Romantic Times* award.

A KISS IN THE DARK
TIFFANY WHITE

Harlequin Books

TORONTO • NEW YORK • LONDON
AMSTERDAM • PARIS • SYDNEY • HAMBURG
STOCKHOLM • ATHENS • TOKYO • MILAN
MADRID • WARSAW • BUDAPEST • AUCKLAND

For Brittany Detmer and Ethan Todd.
Welcome to the world.

Special thanks to Carrie Feron for showing me her slice
of the Big Apple, and to Donna Julian for her connection
to Triple Knight Publishing.

ISBN 0-373-25614-0

A KISS IN THE DARK

Copyright © 1994 by Anna Eberhardt.

Prologue

BRITTANY ASTOR wanted three things:

She wanted to be beautiful.
She wanted Ethan Moss.
She wanted a cat.

The cat was a possibility.

1

BRITTANY ASTOR wriggled her sock-clad feet and stretched. She'd managed to idle away the rainy Sunday morning tucked in bed with the thick weekend edition of the *New York Times*.

Shoving aside the scattered newspaper, she patted the fluffy blue-and-white cabana-stripe comforter in search of the ad she'd clipped from the Positions Available section. Finding the clipping, she fingered it thoughtfully while sipping herbal tea from one of her grandmother's delicate china cups. She read the ad again.

WANTED:
Book Lover with excellent
reading voice. Generous
stipend. 212-555-1130

As a senior editor for Triple Knight Publishing, Brittany knew she more than met the ad's qualifications. She pushed the comforter aside, crawled out of her warm cocoon, and took the clipping to her desk in the living room. The oversize French country desk was a shambles of good intentions. As she placed the ad beside the phone, she glanced guiltily at the slush pile of manuscripts she'd lugged home from the office.

What was she doing, considering taking on a job that required even more reading?

Was she forgetting that it meant extra work—that dreaded four-letter word she tried never to let intrude into her leisure time? One only had to look around her apartment to see that she was more indolent kitten than hyper puppy. Her attitude toward life was that if you moved too fast, things blurred. No one had to tell her to stop and smell the roses.

She loved the sunny, rent-controlled Park Avenue apartment she and her sister had inherited from their grandmother. Francesca, Brittany's older sister, was a globe-trotting model and used the apartment more as a hotel than a home. As a result, the decor was a reflection of Brittany's taste.

The pale yellow living room walls were a pleasing backdrop for her plump, chintz-covered sofas. The large-screen television had Dolby sound, and the kitchen stove was an oversize restaurant model. In the small garden balcony, pastel roses bloomed.

Only one thing was missing from her life—a man to smell the roses with.

One particular man.

Just as seeing a Bengal kitten had put her off wanting any other kitten, so had falling in love with Ethan Moss at the age of fourteen spoiled her appreciation for any other man.

She'd first seen Ethan in Deauville, France, back before her family's fortune had been lost to risky investments. At the time, her father indulged his taste for Thoroughbred racing and had taken the family to Deauville for a vacation, and for the Agence Française yearling sales.

By chance they'd attended the Gold Cup polo tournament, in which Ethan was competing. He and a few of his Argentine pals had won. As she watched Ethan play, sweaty horse and sweaty rider had fused to form an indelible erotic picture in her mind. Man and horse together were grace and power, in control, asserting their courage and skill.

Aside from the sexual rush Ethan's sheer masculine beauty gave her, she was captivated by the obvious joy he took in horsemanship and polo. It wasn't so much the winning he thrilled in, it was the playing.

His exuberant exhibitionism—a primal display of male prowess—had drawn Brittany, the introvert, like a moth to flame.

From that day onward, she'd made it her business to learn everything about Ethan Moss. A New Yorker too, he traveled in her family's set. At first, because Ethan and her sister were closer in age, she'd made Francesca her source of information. Later, when Brittany was old enough, she'd watched him from afar at social events as well as polo matches. They'd been introduced once, but she was sure he would never remember her.

Her heart had broken when he became engaged to one of the "society" beauties. Brittany had almost destroyed the scrapbooks she'd kept on him. When the wedding was abruptly canceled, however, she was glad she hadn't gotten rid of them. Though totally aware of her foolishness, she had slavishly continued to fill the books with articles and pictures.

With a resigned sigh, Brittany set about straightening up her apartment, but the words of the *New York Times* ad never left her mind.

She would answer the ad.

No, she wouldn't.

As she raised the shade at the kitchen window over the sink, she imagined a striped, spotted kitten playfully swatting the tasseled pull. If she got the reading job, she could afford the twelve hundred dollars to buy the designer cat. Then she'd have some company.

She pictured the mystery client—undoubtedly a dowager with a cat . . . some wealthy socialite with poor eyesight. One who'd want Suzy's column in *W* read to her. At the end of the month, the woman would be off to one of her other houses, perhaps in the Hamptons.

Brittany knew all about the rich.

Both she and Francesca had been debutantes. Francesca had been Deb of the Year. Brittany had been relieved just to survive the experience when it was her turn, four years after her sister.

Their mother always referred to the two of them as Beauty and the Brain—she had thought the terms equally complimentary. Francesca, with her glossy dark hair, startling blue eyes and porcelain complexion, was the Beauty. And Brittany, with her light brown hair, most unremarkable hazel eyes and freckles, was the Brain.

It was no surprise that Francesca had gone on to become the Face of the Nineties, a supermodel. Nor was it a surprise that Brittany took refuge in the world of books. Painfully shy, Brittany liked being in the shadows as much as Francesca adored the spotlight. They might have been enemies, but they weren't. They were best friends.

Brittany rubbed her temple. Too much thinking was giving her a headache. She went to the medicine cabinet in the bathroom for a remedy. Chasing the aspirin with a glass of water, she caught her reflection in the mirror.

She was going to be twenty-five in six weeks. She deserved a great present.

She deserved the Bengal kitten.

But treating herself would require moonlighting to get the necessary funds. The ad had said *generous* stipend.

Tomorrow, she promised her reflection in the mirror. She'd answer the ad tomorrow.

"DO YOU WANT TO CALL or should I?"

Brittany looked up from the ad on her desk. She'd been staring at it off and on all day. Now it was quarter to five, and she'd promised herself she'd make the call today. While she wanted the extra money, however, she hated giving up her freedom in the evenings.

"What?" she asked Sandy Christenberry, her petite blond assistant. Why would Sandy want to moonlight? She had a trust fund. The only thing

Sandy wanted, and didn't have, was Brittany's position.

"Lauren Tucker," Sandy explained. "She's not going to be thrilled about this, you know." Sandy waved the sketch in her hand for emphasis.

"Oh." Of course. Sandy was talking about one of Brittany's writers. At the cover conference earlier in the day, Brittany had learned that Lauren's book cover was going to have pink flowers on it . . . lots of them.

"Just fax her the sketch," Brittany replied, ignoring Sandy's look of censure for taking the coward's way out. "Oh, and Sandy," she added, "be sure it's my name you sign to the fax."

Sandy's shrug conceded her temporary defeat. "We'll probably hear her scream all the way from the coast."

"Probably," Brittany agreed. "Close the door on your way out, Sandy. And hold my calls for the rest of the day." Brittany didn't want anyone hearing her making a personal call about moonlighting. Editors weren't supposed to have lives; only careers.

Triple Knight Publishing was a hard/soft publisher. At the moment, Brittany acquired women's fiction and cookbooks. She loved her job, but in publishing the pay left a lot to be desired until you reached the higher echelons.

For now, her rewards weren't monetary. They were the thrill of calling a first-time author and making an offer for her manuscript; the pleasure of seeing a book she'd edited on the bookstore shelves and hopefully on the bestseller lists.

Her ultimate goal was to set the tone of a publishing house as publisher. And to be handsomely rewarded so she might afford to indulge her taste for things like expensive kittens, Broadway plays, maybe even a Thoroughbred of her own.

She'd have a plush office that was custom decorated instead of one filled with posters to cover its dreary beige walls. She glanced around at the piles of manuscripts everywhere, the covers scattered on her desk, the schedule for the year posted on the wall and copies of her books jumbled on the shelf. It was a good thing she wasn't claustrophobic.

Her glance stopped at the ad she'd been avoiding all day. It was time to act.

She punched the telephone number given in the ad, then relaxed back in her chair as she waited for the call to go through. She could hear it ringing. And ringing. Oh, great. The dowager was hard-of-hearing, as well. She wouldn't be reading to the dowager, she'd be shouting.

"Yeah, what is it?"

Brittany was taken aback by the rude male voice that answered.

"Who are you?" she demanded in reaction to his rudeness.

"Dawson, the butler. Who did you want to speak with?" he barked, completely missing her reprimand.

"I'm calling about the ad. The one in the Sunday edition of the *Times*."

"I'm taking care of that. I can give you an appointment with my employer for this evening. You're the first to call. I'll put you down for seven-thirty, and send a taxi to pick you up. What's your name and address?"

"This evening?" Things were moving a little too fast for her.

"Yes, at seven-thirty. Your name—"

The door to her office opened and her assistant called out, advising her that the executive editor, her boss, wanted to see her, pronto.

"Hello..." Dawson said impatiently. "I haven't got all day, lady. The other line is ringing."

"Britt Astor," Brittany replied, adding her address on Park Avenue, while Sandy waved to her frantically.

By the time Brittany fixed the scheduling snafu for her boss and nabbed a seat on the subway, she was too exhausted to worry about the upcoming interview. She was too tired to malinger over the fact that she'd given her name and address to a complete stranger— and a cranky one, at that. Oh, well, the crankiness was actually pacifying. It wasn't as though he'd been dying to get her to come. He'd only seemed annoyed that she was a necessary evil or something—if she'd read his mood correctly.

She closed her eyes and sighed. She might as well nap; there was never anyone all that interesting to look at on the subway, anyway. A few moments later, someone's coughing fit brought her out of her sleepy trance.

The subway car was crowded, and when her eyes blinked open she saw a silver belt buckle on a leather belt cinching a narrow, masculine waist. Glancing downward, she saw jeans-encased legs, then cowboy boots. And not just any cowboy boots; these were tipped with steel ram's heads.

Trying to be discreet, she let her gaze travel back up past the belt buckle to a black leather vest with nothing under it but tanned, sinewy muscle. Inching her gaze higher still, she swallowed dryly at the sight of designer sunglasses, a shock of straight, wheat-colored hair, and a cocky grin.

The last person she'd seen who looked this good was Ethan Moss. And she hadn't seen much of him lately. It was kind of hard worshiping Ethan from afar after he'd fallen from his polo pony during the recent charity match. He'd disappeared from the public eye, the society columns and the tabloids. It seemed he was off nursing either his wounds or his ego—or perhaps both.

She returned her attention to the man in front of her and realized his cocky grin wasn't meant for her, but for the man sitting beside her—a stockbroker type in a fashionable suit and tie. She wasn't disappointed when the hunk got off at the Bloomingdale's stop.

Yeah, she had great taste in impossible men, all right.

SO MUCH FOR HIS IMAGE as a womanizing, jet-set athlete, Ethan Moss thought, sitting alone in the dark.

It had all been a ruse, anyway. He'd been living a lie. The perfect smile that looked out from a hundred newspaper photographs hid a lonely existence.

He'd spent his childhood in expensive boarding schools because his parents were too sociable to be bothered with raising their child. There was always plenty of money, of course. Love was what had been in short supply.

He'd grown into a young man who would take any risk to get the attention he craved. Date any beautiful woman for the same reason. His accident had forced him to see that he'd grown into a man his parents were proud of because he'd become just like them.

He had their superficial values and a life devoid of love. How ironic that the accident that had made him realize the truth had also left him too damaged to pursue love.

No woman would want him now. They would only pity him.

Blind! The pencil in his hand snapped.

He was blind.

Sitting alone in the numbing darkness made him want to swear at the doctors who'd told him there was only a fifty-fifty chance he'd ever see again.

The doctors were fools.

He would see again. *He would.*

He refused to accept any other answer. Or to function as a blind man. That would mean he'd accepted his blindness.

Never.

Which was why he was now hiding in a rented brownstone with his butler-groom, Dawson. He'd had to escape his family's suffocating concern. The flowers, the well-wishers and their whispering had closed in on him like the darkness.

His turbulent feelings, which ranged from fear to rage, had probably alienated all his friends. Only Dawson could put up with him, and even that relationship was tenuous.

He knew he should try to adjust, but he couldn't imagine not living life full tilt. The thought of having to accept that possibility would bring on the dark depression that skirted around him like a night phantom . . . waiting.

"Dawson, where in hell is that Brett guy who's supposed to read to me?" he yelled.

The pealing doorbell was his answer.

"Bring him in here." Ethan shouted the order, picturing a Mister Rogers clone, complete with cardigan. A soft-spoken sort. A pushover.

Finally.

Dawson was determined not to give him the least bit of sympathy. Probably because he wasn't enjoying being pressed into service as a butler, instead of doing his job as groom for Ethan's string of polo ponies.

Mentally Ethan rubbed his hands together, enjoying a sense of power for the first time since his accident.

Bookish sorts were easy to intimidate.

2

AT EXACTLY SEVEN-THIRTY the taxi let Britt out at an imposing residence on East Ninety-fifth Street between Lexington and Park. The expensive four-story residence had arched wood-framed windows and black wrought-iron trim. The front stoop and balconies were decorated with wooden planters trailing greenery.

Very posh. Francesca would say la-di-da, Brittany reflected with a smile.

But it was not anything foreign to her. Wealth didn't intimidate her. And yet her hands were clammy. It was probably the cranky butler, Dawson, who unnerved her.

She reminded herself why she was there. Picturing the kitten that was a cross between an American tabby and the Asian leopard cat, she mentally sharpened her claws. She was shy, but no pussycat. Sandy Christenberry could vouch for that.

Taking a deep breath to steady her nerves, she climbed the front steps to the entrance. She half expected Dawson to answer the door dressed in a tuxedo, but when he appeared he was all jock. A most unlikely butler.

The only formal black-and-white in the foyer was the elegant white marble floor patterned with tiny black diamond shapes. In the middle of the foyer was a large, round, Victorian table. Centered on it was a huge vase of pink peonies. Their sweet fragrance assaulted Brittany as she introduced herself.

"Dawson, was that the door?" a deep voice demanded from the depths of the large, luxurious apartment. "Is it my appointment?"

"Yes—" Dawson began to reply.

"Well, let me get a look at— Oh damn!" Brittany heard the sound of a china cup clattering to the floor. She wasn't certain, but it had sounded as if the cup had been thrown, not dropped.

Dawson, looking more bodyguard than butler, nodded in the direction of the bellowing voice. "You're the first appointment. Let's hope he hires you," he said, leading the way.

Brittany followed in his wake. So much for the dowager she'd fancied. That deep growl belonged to no dowager; it had been ferociously male.

What had she gotten herself into? More important, could she tactfully get herself out of it? Otherwise she'd be stuck with someone like her father, and have to read the sports page and stock exchanges. She'd probably be lucky if cigar smoke and horror fiction didn't figure into the bargain.

"Sir, your appointment is here," Dawson said, showing her to the sofa. Then he exited the dark, richly paneled library, pulling the floor-to-ceiling carved doors closed behind him.

The burgundy leather chair behind the massive desk faced the window, the tall back shielding its occupant from her view. She didn't know what to expect when the chair swiveled to face her.

Whatever her feverish imagination could have conjured up would never have included the man who looked back at her.

For one brief moment before he slipped on a pair of dark glasses, Brittany glimpsed the turbulent emotions on his face. He'd looked utterly lost and alone.

"You're Ethan Moss..." she gasped, identifying the art collector, Broadway-play backer, playboy polo player in hushed surprise.

"You're a woman!" Ethan accused at the sound of her voice.

"Of course, I'm a woman," Brittany declared.

"Dawson said your name was Brett something...."

"You must have misunderstood. It's Britt. My name is Brittany Astor."

There was no reason for him to remember her name. She'd been in love with him forever, but *he* didn't know *her*. Still, it didn't stop the hurt when he didn't respond to her name.

"I don't want a woman," he said with a note of finality. He swiveled his chair back to face the window behind his desk, dismissing her.

"That would be a first," Brittany found herself saying under her breath.

"What was that?" He tilted his head to listen.

"I was merely wondering why you wanted someone to read to you," she said. "Wouldn't Dawson do?"

"Dawson isn't the reading type."

"I am." Brittany wasn't going to be dismissed. She wasn't about to give up easily on what fate had handed her. She fully intended to seize this opportunity to be with Ethan Moss, even if for only one month.

When he didn't comment, she grew bolder.

"What happened? Are you having trouble seeing because of your accident?"

"Yes. Damned Riley threw me in a knock-in. The pony is all right, and I will be in a month or so. Till then, I'm blind. Damned inconvenient," he said, rubbing the side of his head.

Was it true? Brittany wondered. Ethan had said that bit about being blind for *a month* as if he were trying to convince himself most of all. She'd have to ask Dawson. But she'd have to be careful. At the moment, Ethan didn't appear to want anyone's sympathy other than his own.

"How did you know about the accident?" Ethan asked, on a note of suspicion.

"You're a celebrity, of sorts."

"How about you, Miss Astor?"

"I'm not a celebrity. My sister is."

"Your sister?"

"Francesca Astor—the Face of the Nineties."

Ethan whistled. "You must be very beautiful."

"Is it a requirement?"

"It wouldn't hurt...."

"Then I'm beautiful." Brittany suddenly realized those dark glasses were on her side.

"Tell me why I should hire you," Ethan demanded, swiveling around to face her again.

"I'm an editor. You won't find anyone more qualified to read to you." She barely stopped herself from adding, "And I love you."

"I'll want you to read to me every evening for the next four weeks. Isn't that going to cut into your social life? Won't your boyfriend mind?"

"No."

"Why not? I'd sure as hell be upset if my woman were unavailable for an entire month because she was spending her nights reading to a strange man, even if he was blind."

"He's a musician," Brittany invented. "There won't be a problem because he's on tour. He'll be out of town for the month."

"An editor and a musician. Hmm ... an unusual combination. Oh, but I forgot, you're model beautiful. That explains it. We all know rock stars and models are part of the natural order."

Brittany didn't correct her lie. What harm could there be in Ethan's thinking she was beautiful for the month they would share? "Then you're saying I have the job?"

"No, I don't want a woman."

"I'll sue you for sex discrimination."

Ethan sighed. "Why is it that beautiful women are always such a pain? Okay, I'll make you a deal. Read me something. If I like the way you read, you're hired. You can't sue me for not liking the sound of your reading voice."

"What do you want me to read?" she asked, still determined to change his mind.

Ethan shrugged. "You pick something. I don't know what's in this library. I rented the place from a friend of my mother's so I could recuperate in private."

Rising, Brittany walked over to the bookshelves, browsing until she found a book that was suitable. Pulling it from the shelf, she returned and sat, leaning her hip against his desk, emboldened because he couldn't see her.

She began reading from British author Jilly Cooper's massive tome, *Riders*. The gorgeous Rupert Campbell-Black in the story of Olympic equestrian jumping had always been one of her favorite characters, because he reminded her of Ethan.

She thought of the scrapbook clippings and photos she had collected of Ethan since she was fourteen. There was even one treasured picture of him sweaty after a polo game with his arms thrown around the shoulders of herself and Francesca. Of course, it was Francesca he was looking at.

She'd only been a schoolgirl at the time, but she'd never gotten over her crush on him. When she was older, there were the elegant parties. She was sure Ethan didn't remember it, but he'd actually danced with her at her coming-out ball. It was the only thing that had made the excruciating social event bearable. She'd spun out fantasies from that one dance for months.

For years.

But when it had come to him asking one of the Astor sisters out, it was Francesca he pursued. Beauty had won out over the Brain. The fact that Francesca turned him down didn't lessen Brittany's hurt.

But she'd gone on with her life. Or so she'd thought. Her relationships with men, however, never seemed to work out. She always found them lacking... something. Now she wondered if she'd been sabotaging herself by subconsciously comparing every man she became involved with to Ethan. It seemed none of them could ever match him.

Ethan let her read for quite a while before he stopped her. "I guess you thought that was a sure bet, knowing how I feel about horses," he said, sardonically.

"I picked it because it's one of my favorite books," she responded honestly.

"Is it?"

Brittany nodded, then remembered he couldn't see. "Yes, it is."

He ran his hand through his straight blond hair, the action knocking off his glasses. "Damn! I would rather be dead than such a useless wretch. I can't bear the dark prison I've been thrust in. I can't!"

Brittany watched his blue eyes as he felt around on the desk for his glasses, which Brittany saw lying on the floor. She was fairly certain Ethan didn't really need the glasses. They were more likely a prop, a crutch.

"You're hired," he snapped. "See Dawson about the details, unless you've qualms about working for a crazy man."

Brittany realized he'd just hired her to get rid of her because he was embarrassed about being unable to find his glasses.

She didn't stop to pick them up off the floor as she left the room, knowing he wouldn't thank her for that courtesy. He didn't want her help, even if he did need it.

No wonder Dawson was cranky.

And here she was, willingly agreeing to subject herself to Ethan's frustration and dark moods for the next four weeks.

It would certainly test her love for him.

Maybe she would fall out of love with him. Finally.

THE DOORMAN AT Brittany's building let her in when she exited the taxi from Ethan's. Her mind was dizzy from what had happened in the space of the past hour.

She didn't know if it was the elevator making the bottom drop out of her stomach or the fact that she'd be with Ethan for a whole month.

The phone was ringing as she let herself into her apartment. She threw down her keys and leapt to answer it.

"You *are* home. I was beginning to think you were out on a hot date," her sister Francesca teased.

"Where are you?" Brittany asked, not having heard from Francesca since she'd left on a photo assignment for the swimsuit issue of a sports magazine.

"The Côte d'Azur."

"Ah, the fabulous life of a model . . ."

"Yeah, fabulous. The Nice airport is under construction, the traffic is unbelievable and the stores are always closed when I want to shop."

"The Monday flower market, the frankfurters at Voom Voom, not to mention the water-ski instructors at Belles Rives," Brittany countered.

"Okay, Britt, so it ain't so bad," Francesca agreed on a laugh. "Where were you, anyway? Not working late again, I hope."

"I was with Ethan Moss." Brittany couldn't help enjoying tossing that tidbit into the conversation, knowing Francesca would pounce on it like a cat.

"*The* Ethan Moss! *Your* Ethan Moss!" Francesca squealed.

"Don't get excited. It was strictly business. He needs someone to read to him in the evening."

"Britt, little sister, we need to have a talk about come-on lines."

"It's not like that, really. Remember the accident Ethan had?"

"Yeah. Didn't his horse Riley throw him during a polo match?"

"Right. Well, it seems he's suffering from temporary blindness as a result of the trauma."

"Oh, how awful, Britt."

"I know. Anyway, I got the job. Who knows, maybe this way I'll get over him."

Francesca laughed. "Britt, baby, working together is how people fall in love."

"With models, not editors," Brittany countered.

"Tell me that in four weeks, baby sister. Oh, and if you talk to Mom and Dad, tell them to watch for me on the "Fashion Television" show on VH-1 this weekend. The designer line I did is going to be showing. I gotta run. Talk to you later."

Brittany hung up the phone, then sank down onto the sofa to collect her thoughts.

What a difference one little decision could make in a person's life. If she hadn't answered the ad in the *New York Times*, she wouldn't . . . Wouldn't what?

Did she really think this would turn out to be anything more than a temporary part-time job? Just because she had always been in love with Ethan Moss didn't mean this brief association had to lead anywhere.

In a month, her life could return to normal—but would she? Was she risking too much?

Maybe she should just call Ethan and let him off the hook.

No. It was time she moved on with her life. She was almost twenty-five years old. She couldn't go on mooning over Ethan Moss for the rest of her life like some gothic-fiction heroine.

But it was the nineties. Women went after what they wanted in life. And what she wanted was Ethan Moss; blind, or not.

Or was his possible blindness attracting her? She was ashamed to admit its appeal. To admit that it tilted the odds in her favor.

Blind, he believed she was beautiful. Sighted, he would know the truth.

THE FOLLOWING EVENING the taxi Dawson had sent to collect her crawled through the rain-snarled traffic. In the back seat, Brittany tried to assure herself that tonight would be better than her day had been. Sandy had been right: Lauren Tucker had definitely not been thrilled about the pink flowers all over her cover. Both she and her agent had called.

From her bag she slipped the small vial of perfume she'd bought on her lunch hour and pushed the day's problems from her mind. Neither they nor her boss's bad mood were going to ruin her evening with Ethan. Dabbing the perfume, which had promised to turn her into an irresistible seductress, behind her ears and on her wrists, she cast off the gloomy mood the gray, rainy day had brought.

When the taxi stopped at Ethan's residence, she unfurled her umbrella, ignoring the horns of irritated drivers as she made a mad dash across traffic to the entrance. She was successful in getting only a little damp.

After patting her hair, she let herself in with the key Dawson had given her, calling out to announce her arrival. She'd expected Dawson to greet her, but it was Ethan's voice that asked her to join him in the library. Leaving her open umbrella on the marble foyer floor to dry, she entered the room, with ten years of romantic expectations.

"Where—where's Dawson?" she asked, tongue-tied at his sheer magnetism, which seemed to charge the atmosphere in the close room. She told herself she was merely falling victim to the ions in the air. Rainy days always made the scent of another human musky, provocative. And it wasn't as though she wasn't already primed. A harem girl wouldn't be any more ready than she was in Ethan's presence.

"I've given him the evenings off since you're going to be here. You may have noticed he isn't the world's most charming butler. He much prefers being with my polo ponies."

"I wonder why," she muttered under her breath.

"What's that smell?" Ethan wrinkled his nose.

Brittany felt herself blush, the warmth creeping up her face. She'd overdone the perfume.

"I, ah—"

"I liked the scent of your soap much better. Don't wear that perfume again."

She wanted to flee, or melt into the carpet, or just die. Thank heavens he couldn't see her embarrassment. What must he think of her? She should have realized his condition would make him more attuned to scents.

"I tried some perfume on at Bloomingdale's during my lunch hour," she lied, trying to save face. "I won't wear it again."

"Good."

"What would you like me to read?" she asked, grasping for a distraction. "Should I continue with the Jilly Cooper book?" Brittany rubbed her little finger, trying to keep her escalating case of nerves at bay. She felt like a schoolgirl who'd made a terrible gaffe on her first date with an upperclassman.

"No. I'd like you to read this play to me." He shoved the bound manuscript across his desk. "I'm thinking about backing another new play, and this one came to me highly recommended."

As she picked up the script, she took the opportunity to study Ethan.

His appearance was a contradiction. He'd left his white linen shirt unbuttoned, revealing a wide expanse of toned chest decorated with a black cord necklace of small, smooth stones in neutral shades. While the exposure of his bare chest was undeniably sensual, it was a careless sensuality that was an innate part of his unconscious grace.

The dark glasses hiding his blue eyes were another story. They were worn deliberately to conceal. He was hiding from the world—and from her. If it was true that eyes were the mirror of the soul, then he definitely didn't want her to see into his.

When she settled back onto the sofa to begin reading the play, Ethan pushed his swivel chair away from his desk, and rose. "I'll get us something to drink."

"Can I help you?" she asked automatically.

"No. I've familiarized myself with the layout of the rooms. I can get around just fine in my prison without anyone's help. I hired you to read to me, nothing more. I'm not an invalid. I'm a grown man capable of taking care of myself."

Brittany thought he was trying to convince himself more than her, but she said nothing.

"Do you understand?" he demanded.

"Yes, of course."

The awkward moment was diffused by the ringing of the doorbell.

"That will be dinner," he said, heading for the foyer. "I hope you like Chinese."

Brittany had to hold herself in place on the sofa to keep from jumping up to assist Ethan as he made his way through the maze of the room. She held her breath as the oatmeal linen fabric of his pleated trousers brushed against a floor lamp, and it wobbled. When he moved to the foyer to answer the door, she let out a whoosh of relief.

She could hear him talking to the deliveryman as she glanced down at the play, scanning the first page. She heard the door close, and waited expectantly for him to rejoin her.

"Sonovabitch!" The curse was followed by a loud crash.

Brittany jumped up, rushing to the foyer.

Ethan was sprawled on the floor, a look of fury on his face.

"Are you all right?" she asked, kneeling to help him up. "Here, let me help you."

He shoved her hand away. "I think you've *helped* me enough already. What were you thinking, leaving your umbrella in the middle of the foyer for anyone to trip over it!"

"I'm sorry, I didn't think . . ." She dithered, trying to wipe at his stained shirt.

"So much for dinner." Ethan pushed himself up on his feet. "I'm going to change clothes."

Feeling along the wall, Ethan made his way to the staircase on one side of the foyer, moving slowly so as not to slip again on the wet floor.

As he climbed the stairs dripping and scowling, Brittany surveyed the mess her carelessness had wrought. The foyer was a disaster. It looked as though a pair of rambunctious nine-year-olds had engaged in a spirited food fight.

Ethan must have caught the Victorian table to break his fall. In the process he'd knocked over the vase of peonies. The black-and-white marble floor was slick with water from the overturned vase. Peonies were scattered in colorful disarray, mixed with cashew chicken freed from its containers, making the very picture of an exotic dish. The entire tableau was confettied with white rice.

She caught a glimpse of her black umbrella in the corner. It had apparently skittered there, where it rested, looking innocent as a nun.

Brittany sighed. She'd ruined his dinner.

She'd ruined their night. She'd been wrong in the taxi; the evening had gone even worse than her terrible, rotten day.

But she wouldn't give in to her impulse to sit down and cry. While there was a very real possibility that Ethan wouldn't come back down, she couldn't count on it.

She had to right the foyer, return it to order. And do something about dinner.

When she had cleaned up the mess, she went to check the kitchen pantry to see what it offered.

She'd always dreamed of cooking for Ethan. A sensualist, she enjoyed the color, taste, smell and texture of food. In the evenings she unwound from her stressful job by cooking while channel surfing. Then she would read for an hour or two before going to sleep, for both work and pleasure.

Francesca was seldom home, either off traveling for her job, or dating. Brittany seldom dated. She hated it; hated making small talk—and then the awkwardness about kissing at the door.

Trouble was, she was a woman of very definite tastes and she knew her own mind; she was either very interested in someone, as was the case with Ethan, or she wasn't interested at all. She wasn't a flirt like Francesca, who had levels of interest in men that required fractions to define them.

While putting together an impromptu meal, Brittany reviewed the anger and hurt Ethan's behavior toward her had elicited since she'd answered his ad.

She'd secretly hoped for romance, and would have settled for a flirtation.

Instead, Ethan had been rude and unfeeling.

No. *Unfeeling* wasn't the right word. She could overlook his bad behavior because she could only guess at what he was feeling. The emotional pain he was going through had to be devastating.

Before agreeing to take the job, she had questioned Dawson. Badgering him, she'd finally gotten him to admit what she suspected: there was a very real chance Ethan would never see again, and Ethan knew it—even if he wouldn't admit it to anyone, not even himself.

Because of that, Brittany could find it in her heart to continue; to take the abuse because she knew how much he was hurting.

By the time Ethan came back downstairs, she had carried their dinner into the library.

"What's this?" Ethan asked, sniffing the air when he entered the room.

"There's been a slight shift in cultures, but it's the best I could do with what I found on hand."

Ethan didn't comment as she cut into the microwave corn bread, handing him a bite.

"I was in the mood for Chinese," he said, sampling the corn bread nonetheless.

"Well, you're getting Texas chili and corn bread. I've set a place on your desk."

"What's Texas chili?" he asked, easing into the burgundy chair at his desk, and feeling for the spoon beside the bowl of chili steaming before him.

"Francesca had a roommate from Texas who taught her how they eat chili there. Corn chips go in the bottom of the bowl, the chili is layered on the chips, then shredded cheese and chopped onions are sprinkled on top."

"Sounds like I'm not going to get much sleep tonight."

That would make them even, Brittany thought. She hadn't slept a wink last night. Instead she'd lain awake, restlessly thinking of Ethan. Thinking about how she wanted to climb all over him. She had ten years of wanting him stored up inside, but she also wanted to read him the riot act. She wanted to tell him to straighten out; to grow up, and stop being a bear to everyone.

But she'd decided to hold her tongue, and her desires. He'd hired her to read to him. If he wanted her opinion, he'd ask.

Several bites into his chili, Ethan laid down his spoon. "Pretty tasty. You're smart, beautiful, and you can cook. Maybe I should marry you, huh?"

"Huh?"

"Or are you engaged to that musician of yours?"

"About my musician . . . There isn't one," Brittany said, deciding she didn't want any lies between them.

"You broke up?"

"No. I made him up," she said, taking her last bite of chili.

"Why?"

"I don't know," she stalled. She knew. It was because she wanted him to think of her as being model beautiful with musicians at her feet.

"Why don't I begin reading..." she suggested, picking up the play.

BRITTANY FELL ASLEEP within minutes of her head hitting the pillow. Her lack of sleep the night before had taken its toll. She hadn't been asleep long when the phone rang.

She glanced at the digital clock on the VCR. It was past midnight. Her globe-trotting sister, Francesca, never knew what time it was. When she picked up the phone her sister's voice confirmed she was right.

"Do you know what time it is?" Brittany demanded.

"Who cares, Britt. What I want to know is if Ethan Moss is as charming as you thought he'd be."

"Oh yeah, Ethan's a real charmer, all right. How's the shoot going?" she asked, not wanting to think about Ethan the terrible.

"What I wouldn't give for a fine-grained Caribbean beach. The pebbles here are murder to pose on."

"Ah, the hardships of being a supermodel," Brittany mocked, not feeling very sympathetic at midnight with an early-morning editorial meeting looming.

"It does have its compensations. Guess who I'm having dinner with at the Café de Paris tonight? The prince."

"What prince? And what are you doing in Monte Carlo? I thought you were in Nice."

"I'm here to have dinner with the prince."

"Oh. Wow! Really?" Now she was awake.

"Really... But enough about me. I want to know how tonight went." Francesca's voice was full of hopeful suggestion.

"Not great, exactly." Brittany rubbed her eyes, trying to clear her sleep-fogged memory.

"Why? What happened? Maybe it was just the first-date jinx. I do hope you wore something sexy," she coaxed naughtily.

"It wasn't a date," Brittany reminded her. "Anyway, for starters, I left my open umbrella to dry in the foyer."

"Where else would you leave it?"

"*Not* where a blind man could trip over it."

"Oh, was he hurt?"

"Only his pride, I think."

"Oh dear, that's the worst injury for a man."

"Tell me about it."

"So anyway, how did it go after that?"

"He hated my perfume."

"Change perfumes. I wish I'd been there to help you get ready."

"Well, I can't help it if I didn't major in dating in college like you did."

"I did not major in dating. I majored in—ah, okay, so I did major in dating."

"And then Ethan didn't like the dinner I made him. Actually he liked it okay, I guess. It just wasn't what he wanted."

"Baby sister, get a clue. You don't have to major in dating to know men never know what they want. You have to tell them."

"To top the evening off, he didn't like what I read to him," Brittany finished on a roll.

"So read him something else. You're an editor. Pick something you're sure will hold his interest. Read him that scrapbook of press clippings you keep about him."

"Francesca, that's my private scrapbook! How did you—"

"Oh, there's the door. It must be the coach and six the prince sent to fetch me. I've got to quickly find my glass slippers— Bye."

Left with the dial tone, Brittany hung up the phone and lay in bed trying to imagine what it would be like to be beautiful enough to attract a polo player . . . and a prince.

3

SATURDAY MORNING while brushing her teeth, Brittany wondered how much she wanted a gorgeous Bengal kitten. Maybe she should spend her money on a nose job if she really wanted a prince or a polo player.

Bits of conversation as well as reading consumed her evenings with Ethan. She was surprised to find his blindness a liberating experience, making her chatty instead of shy.

While she adored her sister, Brittany had always lived in the shadow of Francesca's great beauty. Everyone noticed Francesca first. They not only noticed Francesca first, but they were so entranced they never looked past her—to see Brittany.

There'd been no way to compete, and so Brittany hadn't tried. She hadn't explored her own possibilities. Instead, she'd retreated to the fantasy world inside her books.

She'd tried to convince herself that Ethan Moss was nothing more than a young girl's fancy—a schoolgirl crush she'd grown past. But seeing him again, suffering as he was, brought long-buried feelings back to the surface.

Apart from Ethan's boorish behavior, which she excused because of his accident, Brittany found being in the company of such a vital, attractive man intoxicating. Especially when she imagined he found her beautiful and interesting.

For the first time in her life she had, in fact, taken to thinking of herself as beautiful. It was only when she was confronted with a mirror, as she was at the moment, that she was dissatisfied.

She decided to act on that dissatisfaction and used Francesca's name to get an appointment at Stephen Knoll's Madison Avenue salon. There she got a sleek new haircut, and an apricot color wash. Going for broke, she also used their makeup services, winding up with what she needed to accomplish softly defined matte lips, and smoky eyes.

Even her assistant complimented her when she arrived for work on Monday.

"Where did you get that suit? It's gorgeous!" But then, being Sandy, she pricked, "Did your sister send it to you?"

"No, I went a little crazy this weekend." The navy crepe suit had a long, pencil-slim skirt with a center slit, which took some getting used to. "Between this suit and my hair, my charge card is still smoking."

"Who is he?" Sandy prompted.

"He?"

"Come on, all this must be for some guy, right?"

Brittany decided she owed it to Sandy to torture her a little. "No. I just thought I'd start dressing for success. Are those my messages?"

Flipping through the slips Sandy handed her, she pulled one out. "Here, you can handle this one, Sandy. I know what she wants. Messenger her an advance reading copy of the new Susann Batson book."

When Sandy left her office, Brittany settled back in her chair.

Would Ethan notice a difference in her? Of course he couldn't *see* her, but she felt more confident. A week had already passed without his acknowledging her as a woman. She had just three weeks left in which to make her dreams come true. Maybe tonight . . .

"I'M BORED."

Brittany set down the play she was reading to Ethan.

"Do you want me to read something else?"

"No. Nothing interests me."

Brittany didn't know if it was her growing confidence from her new look, or the realization that perhaps Ethan wasn't being a jerk because he was blind; that maybe he'd been a jerk all along. Whatever, she was tired of tiptoeing around his peevishness.

"Perhaps we could go to the park," she retorted. "Toss around a Frisbee or something."

"Frisbee! How in the hell am I supposed to toss around a Frisbee? I can't see."

"We could put some of my perfume you don't like on the Frisbee, then you'd be able to catch it."

"So, you think my being blind is funny, do you?"

"No, I think we should talk about it, instead of letting it be the nine-hundred-pound pink elephant we pretend isn't there. Don't you think it's time we talked about it?"

"No."

He swiveled in his burgundy chair so that his back was to her.

Brittany knew from her talk with Dawson that Ethan needed to face the possibility that his blindness might be permanent. She had an idea that might be a step in that direction.

"You know, I think it's time you left your prison," she said, moving to stand beside him. "Time for a scavenger hunt." It was time she stopped humoring him.

"Are you nuts? I hired you to read to me, not be social director on a cruise ship. First it's the Frisbee and now a scavenger hunt—"

"I'll find, you identify," she interrupted, determined to hold her ground. "Unless you think you can't do it. Unless you really do want me to feel sorry for you. Come on, think of it as a goof."

"I don't recall you being so annoying when I hired you."

"Are you coming or do I quit?" She prayed he didn't call her bluff.

"Maybe I'll just fire you," he replied.

"I wouldn't try, if I were you." She was both excited and nervous. Excited to be going one-on-one with Ethan, nervous that she would lose on her one chance.

"Are you threatening me?" He didn't like to be challenged.

"No, but Dawson will. He'll probably kill you if he has to put up with you again in the evenings, as well."

"You're right, he will." His anger dissipated.

"So, are you coming with me?"

"Doesn't look like I have a choice," he said, rising.

The evening breeze teased the budding trees as Brittany hailed a taxi for them. She closed her eyes for a second, to see what Ethan did—nothing but a black void. Opening her eyes, she shook off her sympathy and guided him inside the cab. Following him into the back seat, she instructed the driver to take them to 605 Third Avenue near Thirty-ninth Street.

She settled back next to Ethan. "Give me your wallet," she demanded.

"What? Now you're mugging me?"

"No. You're paying."

Frowning, he handed over his wallet. "Are you at least going to tell me where we're going?"

"No. No clues."

When they arrived at their destination, Brittany paid the driver from Ethan's wallet, and they climbed out of the taxi.

"Just take my arm as though you were a gentleman," she instructed when the taxi pulled away. Brittany then led them inside the Daily Grind where they joined the jostling line at the gray enameled counter.

"Two short, regular, singles," Brittany called out when she got the *barista*'s attention.

Beside her Ethan was quiet. When the *barista* slid their order to her, she handed one container to Ethan, paid, and then they moved toward the door.

"Are you okay?" she asked, noting he looked a little pale.

"Yeah, it's just been a while since I've... Well, I haven't been out in public since..." He shrugged.

"Don't you feel more alive?"

"If tense is alive, then yeah."

"You'll start relaxing," she promised him.

He lifted the container to his lips, tasting the brew.

"Identify," she instructed.

"Well, it's not something that's going to help me relax, that's for sure."

"What is it?"

He took another taste. "Espresso...a full city roast."

"Very good."

"Do I win a prize?"

"The game has just begun. You get five points."

"Oh, goody."

"You could take your shades off, you know," she ventured.

"That's not negotiable."

"Then I take away three points."

"I'm heartbroken," he said sardonically.

"Okay, wise guy, it's your turn."

"My turn?" he asked nervously when she coaxed him outside.

"I hailed the last taxi, you hail this one." The Lighthouse for the Partially Sighted literature had told her not to coddle him.

"I can't hail a taxi."

"How do you know, if you don't try?"

"You didn't say anything about hailing cabs when we started out on this harebrained adventure of yours," he grumbled.

"You didn't ask. Now go ahead and try."

"No."

"You know, I wouldn't have thought a polo player would be such a chicken."

"I'm not chicken. I'm just not certifiable like you. All right, you want me to hail us a taxi? I'll just stand out here in traffic and when one hits me, you can get in," he yelled, stepping down from the curb and waving his hand above his head.

A cab pulled up and braked.

"See how easy that was," she told him, grabbing his arm and dragging him into the taxi.

"You're going to get me killed, do you know that?" he said, sliding across the seat so she could enter.

"No, I'm going to make you live," she countered, giving the driver instructions to take them to Fifth Avenue.

"Give me back my wallet," Ethan demanded.

"What?"

"Fifth Avenue means Saks, which can only mean one thing—a shopping spree."

"Don't be a grouch. I promise I won't buy anything. We're only going to look."

"Brittany, do you really expect me to believe there's a woman alive who can go into Saks with a man's wallet and not buy anything? I'm blind, not stupid."

"You're safe, okay? I had a shopping spree this past weekend."

"Oh? What did you buy?"

"A suit."

"That's it?"

"It's a great suit."

"A bikini?"

"No."

"Good."

What had he meant by that? Brittany wondered, as the taxi neared their destination. They passed a mass of red and yellow flowers in the median, brightening the dusk. She'd started to point them out to Ethan, then stopped herself just in time, remembering he couldn't see them to enjoy them.

She felt a jab of sadness for him.

It was then that she allowed herself to wonder if she could cope even as well as he if she were in his position. She shook off a shudder, unable to think of not being able to read.

"We're here," she announced, paying the taxi. She took his arm, coaxing him inside the expensive department store—and realizing she was enjoying holding on to him just a little too much. They got their share of curious stares from the shoppers they passed. A few women's expressions had been frankly envious.

Brittany had dreamed of being this close to Ethan for so long, and now that she was, she found it addictive. She wanted to savor the scent of his after-shave on his lean jaw, hold on to the warmth of his nearness. Selfishly, she thought how wonderful it would be to have Ethan dependent upon her: not only to have him want her taking his arm, but to need it.

Wants went away, needs did not.

And then she banished the thought, ashamed. She should want Ethan on her terms, not by default. She should want the best for him. And she did, which was why they were heading to the lingerie department. Well, it was one reason.

"Why is it good I didn't buy a bikini?" she blurted out as the salesgirl approaching them was diverted by another customer needing assistance. It wasn't a question she'd meant to ask, but sometimes her curiosity got the better of her, and a question just popped out.

"Because you're a nice girl. Nice girls don't wear bikinis."

"You mean like nice guys don't wear sunglasses at night?"

"Can I help you?" the salesgirl asked.

"No, we're just looking," Brittany answered.

"*You* may be looking," Ethan muttered under his breath.

Brittany didn't give in to the pang of pity she felt. She brought an ivory camisole to Ethan's hand. "Okay, identify this, if you can."

"Are you sure I can't get arrested for fondling the merchandise?"

"I'm sure."

"There isn't anyone watching me, is there? You wouldn't be having fun at a blind man's expense, now, would you?"

"Get a life, Ethan. No one is paying the least bit of attention, hard as that may be for you to believe."

"Why don't I trust you?"

"Okay, so the sunglasses do draw the occasional curious stare. But otherwise . . . nada."

Ethan drew the filmy garment through his hands. "It feels like a camisole to me."

"Two points, but what is it made of? What kind of material? Can you tell me that?" she asked, feeling sexy and daring.

He rubbed the fabric between his long fingers, seemingly lost for a moment. "That's easy. It's silk," he said, refocusing.

"Lucky guess. Okay, five points total."

"Try me again."

"That isn't necessary, you've proved you know your lingerie." Brittany began to think that coaxing Ethan into the lingerie department had not been one of her better ideas. Coaxing Ethan out of it was going to be the more difficult feat.

Ignoring her, Ethan bore out her suspicion and started his mischief. Fumbling around, he plucked a lacy bra from the acrylic display near him. While his choice of lingerie had been random, his words were decidedly not.

"I'd identify this as a 36B.... Am I right?" Ethan asked, dangling it from his finger.

"Give me that," Brittany demanded, snatching it from him, and turning to put it back in place.

"And this feels like lace...."

Brittany wheeled to see him wearing a pair of black lace bikini panties—on his head.

"Ethan!"

"What? They're not lace?" he mocked, humor covering his pain.

"I'm going to kill you," she swore, tugging the panties off his head, tossing them back on the display shelf he'd plucked them from, and determinedly steering him out of the lingerie department.

"How many points do I get?" he asked innocently.

"Ten."

"That makes twenty, what do I win?"

"Wrong. That makes zero. I deducted ten points for that stunt."

"You're not any fun, you know that?"

"Oh, so it's fun you want all of a sudden, is it?" Brittany said, hustling him out of Saks before he could get into any more mischief. "Tell me, what would make you happy this evening—that is, besides wearing lace panties on your head?"

Ethan was quiet for a moment. "There is one thing I've been thinking I would like to do."

"Okay, I'm game—I think."

"I'd really like to see a play."

His request caught her by surprise. Did his commitment to the arts run deeper than the financial investment she'd presumed? Was there more to Ethan than his playboy image would imply?

"Are you sure?" Brittany worried that he might be heading for emotional pain; that he might not be prepared to hear rather than see a play.

"No, I'm not sure, but . . . Let's try it, okay?"

"Okay, what did you have in mind? Something off-Broadway, perhaps?"

"I think I'd like to see *The Will Rogers Follies* at the Palace. We should be able to catch some of it, anyway, if we hurry."

"We'll never get in to see that," Brittany said, relieved. Going to a play was something Ethan ought to give more thought to; it wasn't something he should do on impulse.

"Sure we will, Brittany. I back Broadway plays. They always have room for a backer. Come on, it's your turn to get the taxi."

Ethan proved to be right. They got seats.

Brittany hadn't seen the play before. It was Ethan's second time.

She imagined it must hurt him terribly not to see the sight of the Tony Award-winning spectacle; the rope twirler, the dog act, and the glitzy costumes of the Ziegfield girls.

They held hands and Brittany whispered in his ear, telling him what was happening onstage.

When the musical was over, and they ebbed out of the theater on Broadway and Forty-seventh Street, Ethan was as revved up as the rest of the audience. Maybe more so.

He put his hand on Brittany's as she clung to his arm, guiding him. It felt very much like a date. It was so easy to fall into believing they were a couple.

Ethan held on to her as they waited for the crowd to thin in front of the theater. "This has been—" he sighed "—an evening. Thanks, Brittany."

"But I didn't do anything," she insisted, thrilling to the praise nonetheless.

"Oh, yes, you did. You've been putting up with my awful, dark moods—and I'm not saying there won't be more of them. But tonight—tonight you gave me hope, Brittany. You've been a great pal."

ETHAN LAY ON THE SOFA with an ice pack on his ankle. His high spirits from earlier in the evening were dashed. He had been kidding himself that he could function as well blind as sighted. People responded differently to you when you were handicapped.

Encouraged, he'd gone out after Brittany had brought him home—just out for coffee to celebrate the idea that he could shift his role from athlete to patron of the arts.

In the coffee shop he'd run into friends who hadn't bothered to hide their shock that he was out alone without someone to help him, or their pity that he wasn't the man he'd once been.

And then, on his way from the taxi to the brownstone, he'd slipped on the steps and badly twisted his ankle.

His dreams of functioning as a whole man were dashed. They were as foolish as his dreams that his parents would want him home to celebrate the holidays when he'd been away at boarding school. Each time he'd remained one of the handful of boys who stayed behind for the holidays, his heart had hardened.

He swore at Brittany Astor for chipping away at his defenses enough to give him false hope. He wouldn't be so foolish again. How could he have let that woman wile her way into his life? Couldn't she see he was happy as he was?

UNABLE TO SLEEP, Brittany had taken one of the slush-pile manuscripts to bed with her to read. A few minutes into it, she tossed it aside. It was unfair to the writer to read her work when she herself was in such a major funk.

She was angry at herself, blaming herself.

Ethan would never love her because she wasn't perfect.

And he wouldn't even speak to her again, if he knew what she'd done to him on his wedding day.

The phone rang, jolting her out of her ruminations over her night on the town with Ethan.

"Francesca, you're going to give me insomnia," she complained when she heard her sister's animated voice on the line. "Not to mention that if you don't stop making these transatlantic calls, you're going to wind up in telephone prison."

"Gosh, Britt, you sound like Daddy. Remember when we were teenagers, and he used to make the same dire predictions?"

"Speaking of Daddy, he said to tell you to tell the designers that everyone in Florida hates the grunge look. They caught you on VH-1. I thought you looked great."

"I'll be in South Beach doing some print work this week. Any messages?"

"Yeah, tell Daddy to send money. I went on a shopping spree."

"What did you buy, one of the crocheted hats?"

"No, a suit," she answered, going on to describe it, getting Francesca's approval.

"So, tell me . . ." Francesca said, waiting.

"Tell you what?"

"I called to get an update on you and Ethan, dufus, not to have you give me grief about my phone bill. I can get that from the folks. So how is it going with you and Ethan?"

"Don't ask," Brittany replied, pounding a handy pillow.

"Why? What's wrong?"

"We went out tonight. I wanted to show him he could function and enjoy himself, that he didn't have to stay locked up in his 'prison' as he calls it. I thought we were starting to connect tonight. I thought— Do you know what Ethan called me tonight, Francesca?"

"Not if you don't tell me," Francesca said impatiently.

"Pal!" Brittany wailed. "He told me I was a great pal. What am I going to do? It's hopeless, Francesca. It's never, ever going to work."

"You'll figure it out," Francesca said on a laugh. "I have every faith."

"Yeah, that's what you told me about Latin," Brittany retorted, and picked up her hand mirror. She still had as many freckles as she'd had before the phone rang.

"What about you?" Brittany asked, tossing down the hand mirror, where it bounced on her comforter.

"Me?"

"The prince, remember?"

"Oh, right. I haven't talked to you since then, have I? The prince had lovely manners and he spoke three languages."

"But . . ." Brittany said in the shorthand of sisters.

"But none of the languages he spoke were mine. I'd hate being a princess, anyway. You have to be so pleasant, and public all the time."

"It's just as well. I'd loathe having to call you 'your royal highness.'"

"You're a brat. Listen, I hear the scenery is pretty good in South Beach. Want to join me for a long weekend? We could sponge off the folks, eat key lime pie till we're sick, and whistle at the lifeguards."

"That's politically incorrect, and sounds wonderful but I'll have to pass," Brittany said. As frustrated as she was by the way things were going with Ethan, she wasn't a quitter. And even if she were, this—he— was too important to her. One only got this sort of opportunity at happiness once. "I've got to be Ethan's *pal* to the end of the month," she said, resigned to turning that revolting situation around.

Francesca laughed at Brittany's pique. "In other words, you're not toast yet."

"No, not yet. But what worries me, Francesca, is that I flunked Latin...."

"Don't worry, brat, there's a big difference between Latin and Ethan Moss," Francesca said encouragingly.

"What is that?"

"You didn't really want to learn Latin...."

MORNING CAME TOO quickly.

It was a Tuesday that had Monday written all over it. Brittany looked at her reflection in the mirror while brushing her teeth. She gave herself a foamy grin.

"Hi, *pal.*"

Her reflection stuck its tongue out at her.

"Now is that any way for a senior editor, soon-to-be-publisher, to act?" she asked her reflection.

She really did plan to be a publisher one day. It hadn't been easy making her way up through the ranks, especially since the first company she worked for had folded. But due to diligence, good instincts, a real love of what she did, and luck, she was climbing the ladder to success in the publishing world.

Even if it was too slowly to suit her.

What she craved more than anything was the power to say yes—so much more important than the power to say no.

Brittany finished getting dressed for work, hoping it would be a day without meetings, one when she could shut the door to her office and hide out reading all day.

In her kitchen, she took the time to fix herself a Belgian waffle, topping it with honey and cinnamon. Pouring freshly squeezed orange juice into a crystal goblet, she took her breakfast out to her balcony to enjoy the morning light.

The savory aroma of her breakfast mixed with the sweet fragrance of roses to seduce her into a relaxed state, helping to keep her anxiety about her relationship with Ethan at bay.

Relationship. That was a laugh, she thought, while biting into the airy waffle. The man she was in love with thought of her as a pal. And that was "progress." Romeo and Juliet had had an easier time of it; getting together at least.

The animated noises of a pickup game of basketball drifted up to the balcony; the scuffle of feet, the bouncing ball, and the slang of the street as the players jostled each other, while dreaming big dreams of million-dollar contracts.

Finishing off her waffle, Brittany licked the honey from her fork. A bit of orange pulp caught in her teeth when she drank the last of her juice. She rushed to brush her teeth a final time before heading for the subway.

"YOU'RE LATE!"

Brittany ground her teeth. Sandy, her assistant, had yet to understand what "assist" meant. Instead she spent her time working to undermine her.

"The boss wants to see you," Sandy said gleefully as Brittany set down her things on her desk.

"What about? What's going on?" Brittany had worked in publishing long enough to know things could happen abruptly. Things like firings . . .

"Beats me," Sandy answered. "But she's been looking for you since I got here."

That would be about a half hour, Brittany knew. Sandy got in early—not to work, but to snoop.

Ten minutes later Brittany was back in her office with the door closed, and a manuscript to read. Her boss had handed her the sort of day she'd wished for. The book was up for auction, and they had to decide if they were interested in it, then get back to the agent pronto.

Banishing Ethan from her mind, Brittany opened the manuscript and began reading, wanting what every editor wanted: to be surprised, to be swept away.

And she was.

When she finished reading the manuscript several hours later, she was smiling for more than one reason. The first was that she was going to recommend they make an offer for the book. The second was that she'd found the perfect thing to read to Ethan.

4

BRITTANY FELT ALMOST giddy with anticipation.

It was Friday. On Wednesday, she'd negotiated a good contract for the book. And she'd negotiated drinks with a powerful agent who was hyper to the max.

She was actually humming as she let herself into Ethan's brownstone because she was certain that after tonight, he would no longer think of her as a "pal."

"Why are you in such a good mood?" Ethan asked, as if it were a sin.

Entering the library, she looked to where he sat behind his desk. He used the desk like a shield. Well, it was time she got him to move to a vulnerable place.

"Come lie down on the sofa and relax, and I'll tell you."

"Just tell me. I'm not in the mood to have you play shrink with me."

"Ethan . . ."

"Oh, all right. But no mumbo-jumbo. I've heard all that crap from my doctor. I hired you to read to me, not lecture me." He pushed himself to his feet and made his way, feeling with his legs, to the sofa.

"I am going to read to you. From a book I just bought for my publisher. Stretch out on the sofa and relax," she instructed, taking his chair behind the desk. It was still warm.

"What if I don't like the book?" he asked, throwing off his loafers. "What if it bores me?"

Brittany silenced a sexy giggle, swallowing it. "Be sure and let me know, and I'll stop reading."

"Okay," he said, tucking his hands behind his head and crossing his ankles. "Let's hear it."

Brittany opened the manuscript and explained it was a book of short stories, before she began reading.

"The rain peppered the windshield of my sleek black Jaguar as I pulled up in front of my favorite lingerie boutique. I was late for my appointment with the owner, Alicia, and glad to have my choice of parking spots.

"It appeared no one was out shopping on this nasty fall day. The hothouse warmth of my car was instantly assaulted by damp, chilly air when I opened the door and slid my silk-stockinged legs across the soft leather seat. I made a mad dash through the cold rain for the champagne beige awning covering the shop's entrance."

"Shall I stop? Are you bored?" Brittany asked.
"You've just started," Ethan said, noncommittal. Brittany smiled and continued.

"Reaching the entrance, I pushed against the door to no avail. Deciding the rain had caused the wood to swell and stick, I lunged against the door, only then noticing the Closed sign. The door swung open to my surprise, catching me off-balance and pitching me into the arms of the young man standing just inside the doorway.

"Embarrassed, I began making profuse apologies for my clumsiness.

"'Please, it's my fault entirely,' the young man insisted. 'I'm Alicia's cousin, Benjamin. She had to leave early today and asked me to wait for her last customer. I was just locking up when you didn't show. You *are* Victoria Adams, aren't you?'

"'Yes, I'm sorry I'm late. Traffic was horrible. You know how it gets when it rains in this town.' As I apologized I noticed he wasn't really a stranger; I'd seen him in the boutique from time to time, talking with Alicia.

"Tall, blond and lean, he'd be a hard one to

forget. His blue eyes looked older than his years, which I guessed to be about twenty-nine. It was the way he looked at a woman . . . the savoring appreciation."

Suddenly Brittany didn't feel like giggling. She hadn't counted on how reading the book of short erotic stories aloud to Ethan would affect her. She was starting to feel a flush spread through her body.

"Maybe I should stop—"

"No, no. Continue."

Brittany cleared her throat. There was nothing for her to do but continue.

"Finally he remembered he still held me in his arms and moved to release me. 'You're shivering. How about a cup of tea?' He indicated the silver service on a leather-topped table by the wall.

"'Yes, it would take the chill off.' I'd lied—my shivering had nothing to do with the cold. While he was busy pouring the tea, I walked over to the old-fashioned sofa. When I sat down, I saw he'd been having tea himself and reading while he'd been waiting. There was a half-empty teacup and a paperback novel turned over to mark his place.

"I peeked at the title surreptitiously and felt my

cheeks flame a bright pink. He was reading Victorian erotica, a title familiar to me. The sweet musky fragrance of the boutique seemed to close in, making me feel faint. I was suddenly aware I couldn't sit beside him on the sofa without squirming like a guilty partyer at Sunday church service.

"He walked toward me and the shop's feminine decor made his masculinity stand out in contrast. I'd already noticed more of his physique than was proper—and I was as proper as my name. Unless you counted what went on in my head. But no one could guess that, unless they, too, read Victorian erotica. Oh dear!"

Brittany was silent, biting her bottom lip.
"Continue," Ethan instructed.

She took a sip from the glass of water sitting on Ethan's desk beside the silver pitcher, then read on.

"Benjamin set the cup of tea down in front of me. He must have been napping while he awaited my arrival because he had a slightly rumpled look; his suit jacket was off and his sleeves were rolled up to the elbow. He'd loosened his tie and a trace of five o'clock shadow ghosted his jaw. When he turned to retrieve my order from the

I wasn't sure if I felt relieved or disappointed he'd put some distance between us.

"When he returned with the white box, I jumped up, anxious to leave. 'Thank you for the tea. If you'll just have Alicia put this on my bill, I won't have to hold you up any longer,' I said, reaching for the lingerie box. His large hand covered mine, detaining me.

"'Oh, no. You mustn't leave without trying it on to make sure it fits. Alicia was very explicit about that. She said you're a valued customer and to give you all the time you required. Pay no attention to me. I'll just stay right here and read while you try it on in the attic room.'

"If that was supposed to make me feel better, it didn't! Alicia *was* a stickler for having her expensive, one-of-a-kind designs tried on to assure fit and satisfaction. I could see that Benjamin's mind was made up, so with mounting trepidation I picked up the box and headed for the dressing room that was indeed an attic and the inspiration for the boutique's name.

"Once inside the large dressing room, I forgot all about Benjamin. The room had always had a certain enchantment for me. The walls and eaves were papered with a tiny floral print, and the steamer trunks set about were filled with antique quilts and other treasures, giving the space an air of clandestine privacy. The rain pattering on the windowpanes only added to the atmosphere of a leisurely, stolen evening. On one wall hung a huge floor-to-ceiling painting of a Victorian lady.

"I opened the white box and pulled apart sheer white folds of tissue to reveal the white Victorian gown I'd ordered. Placing the gown on the nearest trunk, I admired its flirty midcalf ruffle as I slipped out of my business suit, revealing my favorite creation of Alicia's—the creamy silk teddy provocatively edged with white ribbon. I slipped out of it and pulled on the Victorian gown. Through the tiny window I could see the rain and fog. I shook off a feeling that I was being watched, but a few seconds later I heard a sound behind me.

"I turned slowly, my heart in my throat. There was no one there.

"Benjamin's voice sliced through the silence as he called upstairs, 'Miss Adams, the mirror's down here. I'm waiting....'"

Brittany looked over at Ethan. He seemed quite comfortable, not fidgeting at all. Maybe this hadn't been such a good idea, she thought, fidgeting herself.

"I'm waiting..." Ethan echoed.

"How could I have forgotten the mirror was downstairs? Now what? I'll have to go down and look at the gown in the mirror. Benjamin will keep insisting. I'll just be quick about it, pretend he's Alicia.

"I started down the stairs after taking a deep, calming breath.

"Benjamin was lounging at the bottom. 'It's lucky I'm a *young* man,' he said, his hand held over his heart protectively. He didn't move, but his blue gaze flowed over me like warm syrup.

"'I find your conduct very unprofessional. Do you flirt with all your customers?' I asked, trying to put some ice into my voice.

"He stood in front of me—his lips a whisper away, his hands hovering mere inches from me in a phantom caress. 'No. Only you. I design the lingerie. Alicia runs the boutique for me. I couldn't resist seeing my design on my favorite customer. The one who buys my most special Victorian creations. You could call it professional curiosity—wanting to see my designs on a flesh-and-blood woman who appreciates them. Or it could just be wanting....' His smile was all silken promise.

"'Which is it?' I had to know.

"He walked over to the sofa and sat down. 'Come here, Miss Victoria Adams,' he ordered softly.

"I was shaken, unable to put a refusal together, much less a coherent thought. Why wasn't I yelling at him, demanding he leave the room? Instead, I felt myself following his command without a will of my own.

"His smile was wide and wicked as I stood facing him. 'How do you feel about temptation, Miss Victoria Adams? Do you ever give in to it?'

"I didn't answer—I barely breathed.

"'Take off the gown,' he ordered.

"The gown slipped to the floor and I stood before him, naked.

"'Tell me, are you a naughty little girl, Miss Victoria Adams?' he asked.

"I closed my eyes.

"'Say it,' he demanded.

"'Yes . . . yes . . . I'm naughty. . . .' I sighed.

"'But only for me, isn't that right?' he insisted, his breathing ragged, his voice needy.

"I nodded my head as if in a trance. 'For you... Only you.'

"It was a thrillingly seductive beginning to our liaison. As it turns out I won't be Miss Victoria Adams much longer; Benjamin is busy designing my trousseau for our honeymoon."

Brittany waited when she'd finished reading. The room was quiet; Ethan's uneven breathing was the only sound.

Finally he spoke.

"You are a very naughty little girl, Miss Brittany Astor.... Aren't you?"

5

SLEEP HADN'T COME EASILY since the accident.

Ethan threw off the covers and tried to get comfortable, balling a pillow beneath his head. Closing his eyes didn't bring the darkness the way it had when he was sighted. Eyes open or eyes closed, the scenery never changed.

What made him more restless tonight was Brittany Astor. She'd knocked the pins out from under him with her stunt earlier this evening—reading erotica to him.

Why had she done it?

That was the question he kept going over in his mind. Cheap thrills? Getting her kicks reading sexy material to a blind man to turn him on? Because she had surely done that.

But somehow he didn't think that was it.

He was fairly certain cheap thrills weren't Brittany Astor's style.

He had a secret. Something he hadn't told her. And now he was glad he hadn't.

He smiled.

Brittany didn't know it, but he remembered her. Sort of.

She was a kid. Or had been in his mind until tonight. She must have been around fourteen when he met her; and he'd been a man, twenty-one. She'd been horse crazy and always hung around his polo ponies. He wondered if the role of tomboy had come naturally to her, or if it had been her way of dealing with being compared to her older sister, Francesca. At that time, Francesca was a stunning eighteen-year-old, and was being courted by photographers.

His mind wandered back to the present. To Brittany now. Why had the minx read the sexy story to him?

Now that he thought about it, it had felt like she'd been baiting him, issuing some sort of challenge.

It was hell not being able to see. Not being able to pick up all the little nuances of social interaction. He didn't like feeling like an outsider.

Her presence seemed to linger in the room... something he found both disturbing and exciting. Was it possible he could have a full life even if his blindness wasn't temporary?

Tonight had been the first real connection he'd experienced since the accident. She'd snuck up on him, and past his defenses. There was something going on between himself and Brittany. He didn't know what, but he was in the game.

His competitive spirit was back.

He'd achieved all his goals by sheer force of will. It was how he'd determined he would regain his sight from the moment he'd learned his possible fate.

He *would* see again.

Because he had to see Brittany.

And then he did something he hadn't done since the accident: He laughed out loud.

He knew exactly what his move would be.

BRITTANY HAD SLEPT like a baby.

It was only when she woke up that she was confronted with misgivings about what she'd done.

Where had she gotten the nerve? And why hadn't she thought as far as the consequences, she wondered for the umpteenth time as she sipped her cup of tea and watched "Style" on CNN. Francesca had gotten her into the habit. The show featured two or three collections by designers around the world, a beauty feature—usually profiling a supermodel like Francesca—and a tour of someone's home.

Normally it was a distracting bit of fantasy. But today, reality superseded fantasy.

She hadn't answered Ethan's question. In fact, she had practically fled his apartment, mumbling something about waiting for an important phone call.

Ethan hadn't believed her, she was sure, but he'd let her escape. Still, tonight she'd have to face him.

A postcard Francesca had sent from Zurich lay on the table. As postcards did, it had arrived after her sister returned. The postcard showed a happy couple dining at the Brasserie Lipp.

The picture brought her thoughts back to Ethan.

She wondered if Ethan was thinking about her. And if he was, what he was thinking.

That she was a brazen hussy? Depraved? Or even worse, ridiculous? At least one thing was certain: he couldn't be looking at her as a "pal" any longer.

What was her next step? Did she make one or wait for Ethan to do something? She couldn't afford to be conservative when she had only two weeks left in which to accomplish what she hadn't done in the ten years since they met.

She wished her sister were here instead of in South Beach. Francesca would be able to advise her about "Now what?"

Francesca was her best friend. Did she envy her? Yes. But Francesca was too generous for Brittany to hate her. Besides, it wasn't as if Francesca had found her prince, and had two cherub-faced children, a cat and a house in the country.

Her sister often joked that she'd kissed more than her share of toads and it was high time she'd found her prince.

Brittany had found her prince at age fourteen. She just had to figure out how to get him to fall in love with her. Getting him to kiss her would be a start. With any luck at all, kissing her had finally occurred to Ethan.

She looked down at her sock-clad feet.

Just thinking about Ethan kissing her made her toes curl.

DAWSON LET HER INTO the brownstone that evening.

"How is he?"

"Unbearable," Dawson grumbled.

Brittany had been afraid of that. Facing Ethan was going to be even worse than she'd thought.

"He's in a rotten mood, then?"

"No. He's annoyingly upbeat. You haven't given him any drugs, have you?"

"Drugs! No. No, of course not."

"Well, whatever it is, he's run my butt all over town today. He's all yours."

Dawson left and Brittany headed for the library, but as she passed the dining room, Ethan's voice stopped her.

"I'm in here."

The flicker of candlelight caught her eye as she turned toward the sound of his voice.

"I hope you haven't eaten yet," Ethan said as she joined him in the dining room.

"I have, actually."

A look of disappointment crossed Ethan's face. "I suppose I should have had Dawson call." He shrugged. "It's just that we'd gotten into the habit of eating dinner together."

"It's Saturday." She'd fallen into the habit of eating with him during the week because it had been more expedient to do so. Often she came straight from her office.

"I suppose it is. Damned thing about being blind is that you lose track of things like that."

"It has nothing to do with being blind. It has to do with you withdrawing here, hiding from the world and living one day much like any other."

He didn't argue with her. "Sit down and keep me company while I eat—and make sure the candles don't set the place on fire. I'd hate to light my own funeral pyre."

Brittany took the seat to his left where a place had been laid for her on the gleaming cherrywood table. Candlelight warmed the dark forest green walls and rich colors of the Oriental rug. An oil canvas of a Parisian scene hung on the wall behind Ethan.

"Tell me about your day," he said, twisting the herbed angel-hair pasta in his plate around his fork.

He was acting as if nothing had happened. As if she hadn't read him something surprising. Well, she certainly wasn't going to bring it up, though she couldn't believe he was going to let what had happened pass without comment.

"I spent the day listening to myself," she answered.

"You talk to yourself?"

"No, I listen."

He looked puzzled.

She explained, watching him work at getting the pasta onto his fork. "I have this ritual I do on weekends. On Saturday morning I watch 'Style' on CNN and on Sunday morning I read the *New York Times*. Then after that I don't do any more input. I spend the rest of the day listening to myself . . . dreaming, pretending, imagining, inventing, fantasi— Uh, you know, finding out who you are, making friends with yourself."

"You just sit and do that?"

"Sometimes. Sometimes I bake, sometimes I clean, and sometimes I putter with my roses on my balcony garden."

"You must have been an odd kid," he said, giving up on the pasta and buttering a roll.

"I was a kid who got lost in books. It's why I became an editor. I love ideas."

He took a bite of his roll and chewed it thoughtfully. "So that's what you did when you were a kid? You read books?"

"That and rode horses. How about you?" she asked, anxious to turn the conversation away from herself.

"I rode horses, too," he said, making another stab at getting the angel-hair pasta from his plate to his mouth.

That he'd done in spades, Brittany reflected, a thousand images of him doing just that imprinted on her mind. She sat across from him, staring, drinking in his masculine beauty. Splashed with golden candlelight, he had an almost-mythical aura.

The fourteen-year-old in her was swooning. The twenty-four-year-old stilled his hand. "Let me help you," she offered, taking his fork.

"What, no 'You have to learn to do this on your own' crap? Have you finally accepted that I'm not going to be permanently blind?" he asked, letting her feed him.

"I haven't accepted anything. If your sight doesn't return, I'm not the one qualified to help you adjust to it. I can only show you that you can deal with it—that life is worth living."

"Oh, that's rich, coming from someone like you who hides from life in the world of books."

She shoved a forkful of pasta to his lips, wanting to silence words she'd heard all too often from Francesca.

The silence stretched out before them as she fed him. It only served to accentuate their intimacy. Growing nervous, Brittany offered up a rebuttal. "Everyone is different. Some people seize life as you always have. Others, like me, flow with it."

"In other words, whatever floats your boat..."

"You could say that, yes."

Ethan pushed back his plate. "I've had enough pasta. If I eat any more, I'll be too full to enjoy dessert. You will share dessert with me, won't you?"

"Unless it's cheesecake," she agreed. "I think I must be the only person in the world who doesn't like cheesecake."

"In New York, anyway," Ethan said with a chuckle. "I think it's a hanging offense in New York, isn't it? After all, New York cheesecake has a claim on culinary fame."

Brittany made a gentle stab at the back of his hand with her fork. "Promise you won't tell...."

"Promise, if you'll get dessert from the kitchen. It's in the fridge."

Brittany collected the dinner china and silver, carrying it out to the kitchen sink. She was glad of a chance to be alone, to try and figure out how she was doing.

Of course, she was clueless. Ethan was flirting with her, but only casually, the way he'd naturally flirt with any woman from two to ninety.

And while he wasn't quarrelsome or being a jerk, he also wasn't showing any real response to the sensual gauntlet she'd tossed down between them in the form of the erotic story she'd read to him.

Opening the refrigerator, she groaned at her ineptitude when it came to seduction. Ethan probably thought she was stupid. He was ten years older; more worldly, and certainly more experienced.

Francesca couldn't come back to New York soon enough. By her sister's return tomorrow night, Brittany was afraid she'd have screwed up irretrievably her one chance with Ethan.

She reached past the bottled water on the top shelf of the refrigerator to the square white box. It was very light—definitely not cheesecake. With his sophistication, Ethan would be the type to prefer fancy European puff pastry—and not a mousy book editor.

Only he could turn her confidence to dust like this, she thought, telling herself to snap out of it.

"Did you find it?" Ethan asked, when she finally returned to the dining room.

"Got it." She set the box down in front of him.

He pushed it toward her. "You open it."

Brittany took her seat and reached for the box. He was probably afraid of squishing the dessert.

She slipped the silver cord from the white box and opened the lid.

"Do you like it?"

Brittany was silent a moment. "It is cheesecake, after all," she said finally, surveying it.

"I never said it wasn't."

"Where did you get it?"

"I had Dawson take me, grumbling all the way. Well, he drove me. He refused to come inside Saks with me."

"So what did you do, tell the saleslady what you wanted and let her select one for you?"

"Yes. She remembered me from when you took me there. I told her it was for you."

Brittany lifted the "dessert" from the box. She let the black stretch lace chemise dangle from her finger.

"What do you expect me to do with this?"

"Why, wear it, of course."

"Wear it?"

"Yes, I'm going into the library now. You can change into it and join me there."

"But you can see right through it!"

"No, actually I can't. But I can use my imagination. You know, like you do. So go ahead and change. I'll be waiting for you to read me another story."

With that, Ethan got up and made his way from the room to the hall. She could hear his footsteps on the marble floor as he made his way to the library to wait for her.

He certainly had picked up the gauntlet. And tossed it right back into her court. Now what?

"I'm waiting..." Ethan called from the library.

Well, was she a gutless wonder? A woman or a mouse?

She picked up the scrap of lacy fabric, eyeing it speculatively. Ethan had said he couldn't see her, and that was true enough. So she could do this because, after all, he believed she was beautiful. She'd told him so herself.

Gathering up her courage, she carried the chemise with her to the library where Ethan waited.

"You've changed, then?" He was behind his desk again. Confident and in control.

"No. I thought I'd do it in here so you could enjoy using your imagination."

He didn't comment.

"I have just one question," she said, laying the chemise on the back of the sofa while she stepped out of her shoes.

"Okay," he agreed.

"Why? Why the lingerie?"

His laugh was low and sexy. "I thought it only fair to warn you that I don't play fair, either."

"Oh."

Brittany's hands shook as she undid the top button on her favorite weekend outfit. It was an easy Empire-waist tank dress of lightly crinkled cotton. The style was relaxed and it buttoned from neck to hem.

She finished with the buttons, letting the dress slide to the floor. But she didn't, couldn't, look at him.

Then she picked up the chemise.

"Uh-uh. Take off your underwear," he instructed.

"Maybe I'm not wearing any," she countered, annoyed with him, yet pleased he was developing his other senses. Even if he believed his sight would return, he was learning ways of coping unconsciously that would aid him if it didn't.

"Are you sure you can't see?" she demanded, his silence making her very nervous.

"I'm certain. As you're a book editor, it's not far-fetched to imagine you would be wearing under-wear—am I right?"

She mumbled something under her breath while stripping down. Naked, she pulled on the lacy che-mise. The bit of froth was meant to display what it covered and only served to make her feel more na-ked. It skimmed her body to graze the tops of her thighs. Slim straps crossed in back, the neckline scooped low in front and the sides were slit.

"The least you could do is loosen your tie," she said.

He obliged her. It only made him look sexier.

"I'd like it if you stretched out on the sofa while you read to me."

"Any more instructions?" she asked, petulantly.

"Since you asked. I'd like it if you'd stretch out on your stomach on the sofa while you read to me."

"On my stomach . . . ?"

He shrugged. "It's an image I get."

It was an easy enough request to honor. Reading him a story was a problem, however.

She'd forgotten to bring the book.

Her mind cast about frantically for a few seconds until she hit upon a solution to her dilemma.

"I'll be right back."

"Where are you going?"

"I left the book on the entry table, and I need to get it," she said, improvising.

When she returned to the library she carried one of the oversize hardback picture books she'd recalled seeing on the foyer table. Ethan wouldn't know the difference. He'd only hear her turning the pages. All she had to do was make up a bit of erotica to please him.

Right. A new wave of nerves hit her as she stretched out on the sofa on her stomach as Ethan had instructed and opened the book.

She heard Ethan help himself to a drink of water from the silver pitcher on his desk as she frantically searched for inspiration, flipping through the picture book. The book wasn't much help. It was a study of the architecture of college campuses.

Inspiration finally struck when she turned the page and saw a coed at an introductory tea in the dean's office.

"I'm waiting . . ." Ethan prompted.

Brittany took a deep breath, tried to forget what she was barely dressed in, and who she was with. She closed her eyes and began "reading."

"It's November, halfway through freshman year. I'm transferring to West Lewis College, a small girls' school on the East Coast.

"When I arrive at the dean's office to register, his secretary informs me there has been a scheduling mix-up. The dean is having a tea for the mothers at his home. She sends me to his on-campus residence to wait for him.

"When I arrive at his large Victorian brownstone, his housekeeper shows me to his study to wait, telling me it will be about a half hour until the tea is over.

"His study is cluttered with paintings, statues and plants. The walls are dark, the sofa and piano bench covered in burgundy velvet. I can hear the chatter of women in the parlor, as the housekeeper has left the door ajar.

"I select an Edith Wharton biography to read. The fireplace is lit and I find the room warm. I shrug off my blue uniform blazer and lay it on the piano bench. My white blouse has come untucked, so I shove it back inside the waist of the green-and-blue plaid pleated skirt that matches my school blazer. After tugging up my white knee socks, I toe off my loafers and stretch out on the velvet sofa on my stomach and open the book to read.

"As I read, I can hear the dean's deep voice mixed in with the women's high voices. But as I get caught up in the book, the voices drift away.

"After I read a few chapters of the biography, I realize Edith Wharton interests me enough that I consider doing a paper on her for my freshman writing class.

"When I return to chapter four, I hear a door I hadn't noticed on the other side of the room behind me open. Since I can still hear voices in the parlor, I know the tea isn't over. It's too early for that, at any rate. I am about to look over my shoulder to see who has joined me, when a low whispered command stops me: 'Don't look up . . . just keep reading.'

"The authority in the male voice brooks no objection, so I obey. I return to my reading, not looking up even when I feel the man's hands move my legs so that he can sit down on the sofa.

"The words on the page blur in front of me a few seconds later when I feel his long forefinger hook the edge of my knee-high sock and tug it down to bunch at my ankle. I draw a quick intake of breath when I feel warm breath on the back of my knee and the lingering sensual kiss that follows. Tremors of desire creep up my thighs. I shouldn't allow this—I shouldn't. This is bad. *I'm* bad if . . .

"The log in the fireplace shifts, falling in a crackle of sparks in the warm, hushed room. I can smell the faintest hint of after-shave. What if the housekeeper returns! I do nothing. Just wait.

"My eyes close tightly, banishing guilt as I allow the hand that inches up my pleated skirt to reveal my white cotton panties to him. I can feel his eyes gazing, and then his hand smoothing over the taut cotton . . . his finger trailing along the elastic edges suggestively.

"I quiver, and start to look over my shoulder. His hand shoots out and tugs my ponytail, arching my neck backward, holding me firmly. 'Keep reading,' the low voice pleads. 'Don't take notice of what is happening. I only want to please you. Understand, young lady?'

"He releases my ponytail and I nod, returning to my book. I turn the page, managing to read the first paragraph before being distracted by his hand slipping beneath my abdomen.

"I freeze when I hear footsteps but they go past the door. 'Lift up . . . just a little . . . . Yes, like that,' he urges. He begins peeling my panties down from my waist, tugging them to my knees.

"My face flushes to have a stranger—to be exposed so— I begin to lower my stomach to the velvet sofa to hide....

"'No, no. You must not hide from me,' he instructs, sliding his hands beneath my hips to lift me until I am braced on my knees and elbows.

"'Very nice. Now dip your back, young lady, and continue reading while you display yourself to me.' His hand pushes insistently on the small of my back. I obey, caught up in a wanton fog.

"I feel his hand smooth the insides of my thighs, spreading them apart a bit more. My breathing is shallow. The room has become a hothouse. The velvet sofa beneath my elbows cushions my arms as I try to continue holding the book. Reading it is impossible.

"When I feel his soft, blowing breaths on my damp curls, I clamp my lips together tightly, fighting the urge to do the same with my legs as he teases. I drop the book when he closes his mouth over my pulsing need, beginning a slow, sucking kiss as his thumbs separate and hold me in place for him until the room begins to spin. I bite my lip to stifle my cry of pleasure as I come against his mouth.

"Moments later, I realize I haven't heard the dean's deep voice amid the women's chatter for some time.

"Had he been called away from the tea to handle something urgent—in the study . . . ?

"I hide my face in the sofa pillow as I hear the stranger leave the room."

Brittany opened her eyes, blinking out of the sensual trance she'd slipped into. She stared at the picture book she still held, realizing she'd forgotten to turn the pages. Had Ethan noticed?

He was very quiet.

What was he thinking? Had she gone too far?

Finally he broke the silence. "What made you do it?"

So he had noticed she hadn't been turning the pages of the book. She repeated his question, stalling for time, "What made me do it?"

"What made you decide to read erotica to me in the first place?"

He *hadn't* noticed she'd made up the fantasy, she understood with a sigh of relief. Nevertheless, that didn't make his question any easier to answer. There was no way she could tell him the truth—that she'd deliberately set out to seduce him into thinking of her as a woman instead of a "pal."

So she lied.

"I read somewhere that people with phobias about flying were encouraged to take erotica along to read during flight as a distraction from their fears."

"I'm certainly not afraid to fly."

"I know. You're an international stud." She could have bitten her tongue for that slip. "I read it because you are afraid."

"I'm not afraid of anything," he said obstinately.

"I think you are."

"Well, you're wrong."

"Then why are you refusing to even consider the fact that you may indeed be permanently blind?"

"I think it's time we called it a night," he replied, dismissing her, obviously not wanting to discuss his blindness.

"I think it's time you faced the truth," she insisted.

"Good night, Miss Astor."

"You're sending me home?"

"Yes."

"Do you mind if I dress before I go? Or have you forgotten I'm practically naked . . . ?"

"Oh, no. I haven't forgotten. Let's just consider tonight a draw."

6

ETHAN PACED THE apartment late into the night. He'd finally come to stand before the floor-to-ceiling windows where he'd been for the past half hour, staring out sightlessly from force of habit.

Brittany was right. He was afraid.

He'd thought by now his sight would have returned. The few weeks since the accident had stretched to seem like a year. By now he should be seeing light and shadow, shouldn't he?

Something, anything.

He was afraid to ask the doctor. Afraid the doctor would confirm his worst fears—that his sight wasn't going to return, *ever*.

He slammed his hand on the window frame, allowing himself the indulgence of his feelings—his true feelings—now that he was alone.

A cry of mental anguish escaped his lips and he clamped his eyes shut. But he couldn't shut out the reality or stop the flood of tears.

Turning from the window, he returned to the library where he threw himself down on the sofa, emotionally exhausted from confronting his demons. He'd taken so much for granted—the privilege and the passions of his life.

Brittany's scent was on the sofa pillow. Inhaling it, he felt his mood lift. He pictured her lying on the sofa—first in the bit of lingerie he'd bought her, then in the schoolgirl uniform of the fantasy she'd read to him.

Oh, yes, he felt much better.

Well, hornier, anyway.

He smiled. What would he have done without Brittany? Without her to challenge him, he would surely have gone mad by now. What was a beautiful career woman like her doing spending her leisure time reading to him? He hadn't asked her why she'd wanted the job. He'd have to rectify that when he saw her again on Monday evening.

Had reading the erotica to him affected her, too? He sensed that despite her daring, she was shy. He wondered what kind of woman the freckled, horse-crazy young girl had grown into.

If only he could see.

He felt around on the end table until his hand came in contact with the remote control. Picking it up, he flicked on the TV, surfing the channels until he heard a familiar voice. Somehow he no longer felt like being alone. Lulled by the comfort of the TV, he drifted into the embrace of sleep.

In his dreams he could do all the old things—ride his polo ponies at breakneck speed, drive his sports cars around hairpin turns . . . *see.*

The aroma of fresh coffee woke him—French vanilla. He recognized Dawson's heavy tread on the carpet. It was true that his other senses had heightened to make up for his lack of sight.

At the rattle of cups when Dawson set the tray down on the coffee table, Ethan pushed himself into a sitting position on the sofa. "Dawson, why are you bringing me coffee in the middle of the night?"

"It's almost noon."

"Why didn't you wake me when you came in?"

"You looked comfortable."

"Oh." Ethan rubbed his hands through his hair. The last thing he remembered was a freckled Lucy Ricardo asking him how long he'd been dean of the university.

Boy, did he need coffee! He took the cup Dawson set before him.

He drank down the steaming liquid and waited for the caffeine to kick in as Dawson brought him up-to-date on his polo ponies.

"You know what I want to do today, Dawson?" he asked when Dawson finished.

"Go to the stables?"

"No. I thought we'd go shopping."

"Shopping," Dawson repeated without enthusiasm.

"Shopping."

"Saks?" Dawson inquired, resigned.

"Saks."

"But this time I'm going to need your help, Dawson."

"What about Miss Astor?"

"What about her?"

"Couldn't she take you shopping?" Dawson asked hopefully.

"No. I want this to be a surprise."

BRITTANY PUSHED THE spiderweb away from her face, but it kept drifting back. She swatted at it again. And again, grumbling.

Francesca's giggle woke her.

Brittany blinked open her eyes to see her sister kneeling on the edge of the bed, the black lace chemise Ethan had bought Brittany dangling from her forefinger.

"You want to tell me about this, baby sister?" Francesca said. "And I do hope Ethan Moss figures somewhere in the explanation."

Brittany yawned, pushing herself up against the mound of pillows at her headboard. She rubbed her hands over her eyes sleepily. "When did you get in?"

"I think the more interesting question here is, when did you?"

"Will you please put that down!" Brittany lunged for the scrap of black lace Francesca seemed intent on waving like a flag.

Laughing, Francesca stepped just out of reach. "Uh-uh. Not until you tell me how my baby sister, who wears socks to bed, happens to have this bit of racy lingerie."

"Would you believe I bought it?" Brittany asked on a hopeful note.

"Nope. Come on, give."

Brittany shoved her covers back. "Oh, for heaven's sake, Francesca, I haven't even had my coffee yet."

"Okay, we'll talk over coffee," Francesca acquiesced, tossing the chemise over a chair. "But I want details."

Brittany groaned, then schlepped to the kitchen in her socks and oversize T-shirt. Francesca chattered as Brittany ground fresh coffee beans, the full-flavored aroma giving the room a mouth-watering smell.

Brittany rinsed the gold coffee filter, added the ground coffee and water to the German coffeemaker, then dug up a tin of shortbread fingers while listening to Francesca's animated retelling of her visit with their folks.

"I came back a day early because Mom and Dad were making me crazy. Dad with his portfolio advice, as if I were any better at holding on to money than he is. And Mom—all she wanted to know was when I was going to quit all this running around the world to settle down and give them grandbabies."

Brittany laughed, setting out cream and sugar.

"Grandbabies, I tell you," Francesca said with a roll of her blue eyes. "This from a woman who never saw me in a school play."

"Well, it is your duty. You are the oldest daughter, you know. And you're not getting any younger," Brittany added with a grin. She poured the steaming coffee, relieved the conversation had drifted from the black lace chemise and its origin.

"Don't remind me. I can't believe I'm already twenty-eight years old. Twenty-eight is practically ancient for a model. Model years are like dog years. And all these new waif models coming up behind me look like absolute babies."

"Twenty-eight isn't old for a model anymore, Francesca." She offered her sister a shortbread. "Look at Lauren Hutton."

Francesca shrugged at the mention of the fifty-year-old model and passed on the cookie. "No sweets, I have a shoot in the morning."

"Oh, come on, have a cookie. You're so beautiful, a zit would give you character." Brittany waved the sweet under Francesca's perfect nose.

"You've got to be kidding. I have to be as flawless as I can to even have a hope of snaring a cover on this shoot."

"So it's for a magazine. What is it, the swimsuit edition of *Sports Illustrated?*"

"Don't I wish. No, it's for *Rolling Stone.* They're doing a feature on rock stars and models; you know, Mick and Jerry, Rod and Rachel . . ."

Brittany looked puzzled. "But they're all married."

"I know. My agent informed me they decided to throw in a single guy for good measure. I get to pose with him."

"Who is he, do you know?" Brittany took a bite of her shortbread.

"Tucker Gable."

"Tucker Gable!" Brittany choked.

"Yeah. Everyone figured he and Chelsea Stone would tie the knot eventually before Dakota Law stole her from under his nose. Now he's rock's most eligible bachelor."

Brittany grinned.

"What?" Francesca sipped her coffee.

"I was just thinking maybe Mom won't have to wait for grandbabies much longer."

"Oh, please. Another model and a rock star. I don't think so. It's just too trite."

"Uh-huh." Brittany topped off their coffee cups and began humming, "Dum . . . dum . . . da . . . dum . . ."

"Will you quit with the 'Wedding March'! Let's get back to discussing you. So tell me, where did that naughty nightie come from?"

"Saks."

Francesca shook her head. "That's not what I asked."

Brittany knew her sister wouldn't quit until she had the details. Francesca had their mother's tenacity. There was nothing for Brittany to do but give in and tell Francesca what she wanted to know. One way or another, she would worm it out of her eventually.

Brittany set down her coffee cup with a sigh of resignation. "Ethan gave it to me, okay?"

"More than okay." Francesca let her wrist go limp and shook her hand in a gesture of sisterly approval. "Way to go, baby sister."

"No. You don't understand. It was his idea."

"Even better. So-o-o . . ."

"So what?"

"So give. Have you worn it for him yet?"

"Well, yes. But—"

"All right!" Francesca squealed.

"Calm down. It's not what you think. Ethan can't see, remember."

"So, that doesn't mean he can't—"

"Francesca!"

"Oh, for heaven's sake. No wonder you love all those Victorian novels. You act like a Victorian heroine. Don't tell me the two of you are playing *The Age of Innocence* game. All looking and no touching."

"I told you he can't see."

"So you are touching, good."

"We're *not* touching."

"No looking? No touching? So what exactly are the two of you doing?"

"I don't know exactly."

Francesca took Brittany's coffee cup and set it with hers on the counter, then tugged her sister into the living room and sat her down on the chintz sofa beside her.

"Tell me what you do know."

"Ethan doesn't think of me as a pal anymore," Brittany ventured.

"And why is that?"

Brittany swallowed dryly. She and her sister had always shared confidences, but she didn't know about this....

"I'm waiting," Francesca said, reaching for the Sunday edition of the *New York Times* on the coffee table. She tossed the *Book Review* to Brittany automatically, then pulled out the travel section for herself.

Brittany glanced absently through the hardback bestseller list while Francesca scanned the travel ads. Lawyers were starting to appear on the book lists more often than in court.

Tossing the newspaper aside, Brittany tried to explain to her sister what was happening. "You know I answered the ad in the *Times* Ethan placed for someone to read to him. Of course, I didn't know it was Ethan's ad. I just wanted to earn some extra money to buy a cat. Don't you think it would be great having a cat in the apartment?"

Francesca looked up from the ad she was studying. "Why, do we have mice?"

"No. I meant for companionship."

"Companionship? I'd even take Tucker Gable over a cat for companionship. I thought you had Ethan for that now. Let's get back to the part about why Ethan doesn't think of you as a pal any longer."

Brittany undid her ponytail and rubbed her hands through her hair to relax her scalp. "Well, at first I read him a Jilly Cooper book. Then he wanted me to read him a play he was considering backing."

"This is when he thought of you as a pal."

"Right."

"What happened to change that?" Francesca asked, tossing down the newspaper.

"Last week Triple Knight had to decide if they wanted to bid on a manuscript a top agent was conducting an auction on. My boss gave the manuscript to me to read to see if we were interested."

"Hey, how's that—" Francesca snapped her fingers trying to recall a name "—that Sandy person doing? Your assistant who keeps trying to steal your job. Is she still trying to undermine you?"

"She's ambitious. You can't blame her for trying."

"I can if she's trying to steal my baby sister's job," Francesca said.

"I can take care of myself."

"That's not what the doorman tells me. He says you're an easy touch for a handout. Sometimes I don't know how you survive in New York."

"And I think I've got a mother everywhere I turn," Brittany countered. "Maybe that's why I did what I did."

Francesca's eyes narrowed. "What did you do?"

"I read the manuscript—or some of it, at least—to Ethan."

"What's wrong with that? Is it illegal or something?"

Brittany shook her head no. "We own the manuscript. But the book is . . . It's a book of erotica."

Francesca's mouth dropped open. "What did Ethan say? What did he do?"

"The first time I read—"

"Whoa! The first time?" Francesca threw up her arms and grinned. "He liked it, huh? It's ongoing, then? That's what the two of you have been up to?"

Brittany nodded. She wasn't ready—might never be ready—to tell Francesca she'd made up the second fantasy she'd "read" to Ethan. One had to keep *some* secrets. Although, after having shared a fantasy with Ethan, she hardly had any secrets from him.

No, that wasn't entirely true. She did have a secret from Ethan. A very big secret.

A secret he knew nothing about.

Couldn't know about.

Not ever.

He'd never forgive what she'd done.

"IT'S YOUR MOTHER," Dawson said. "Shall I tell her you're sleeping?"

"No, I'll take it." Ethan was in such a good mood that even his mother's hovering couldn't bring him down. His shopping had gone well. He was looking forward to Brittany's visit tomorrow night.

She had managed to lighten his heavy heart—something he hadn't thought possible without his sight returning.

Now he was beginning to believe he could survive the loss of his sight—if he had Brittany by his side.

Taking a deep breath, Ethan picked up the phone.

"Hello, Mother."

"Ethan. Are you all right? I've been calling you all afternoon. Where have you been? Your father and I have been so worried about you."

"I'm fine, Mother. Dawson and I went shopping."

"Shopping. Are you sure that's wise? If you'd only asked, I would have sent you anything you needed."

"I know, Mother."

"What were you shopping for, dear?"

"Ah, just some personal stuff."

As his mother relayed family news, Ethan's attention wandered to Brittany and his successful shopping trip. He wondered if he was being foolhardy.

Maybe he was just mistaking pity for something more.

He shook off the unwelcome thought, and let his mother's voice drone on as more pleasant thoughts of Brittany filled his mind.

"YOU HAVEN'T SAID whether Ethan is a good kisser," Francesca prompted.

"That's because I don't know," Brittany replied, taking off her brimmed hat and hanging it on the entry hat rack.

"You don't?"

"What did you think about the new Barnes & Noble superstore?" she asked, changing the subject to the bookstore they'd just cruised. "Is it great or what?"

"It's great," Francesca agreed. "What's not to like about a three-story meat market?"

"That's only the cappuccino sippers on the mezzanine. Most of the people in the store were looking for a good book to read. What did you buy?" she asked, taking the Barnes & Noble bag from her sister and peering inside.

"A Nathaniel Hawthorne mug." Francesca untied her long-sleeved striped T-shirt from around her waist.

"Only you would browse a 30,000-square-foot bookstore and come out with a mug."

"I like Nathaniel Hawthorne."

"*You* like Nathaniel Hawthorne?"

"Yeah. What was it he said? 'Easy reading is damned hard writing,' or something like that."

"And here I thought you slept through lit class."

"Nope. There was this dreamy guy named Steve in my lit class. He liked Nathaniel Hawthorne," Francesca explained, her blue eyes twinkling.

"You're a hopeless case."

"Brittany..." Francesca said, suddenly sounding serious.

"What is it?"

"How is Ethan, really? It must be pretty traumatic losing your sight like that. Is there a chance he will see again?"

"The doctor said it was possible. He has a fifty-fifty chance. But Dawson said the odds go down as time goes by."

"You sure you know what you're doing, baby sister?"

"I know," she lied. She didn't know anything other than that she had to take the chance she'd been given; had to risk having her heart broken.

"Brittany..."

"No more questions. I've got to read this manuscript by morning," Brittany said, picking it up from the corner of her crowded desk.

"Just one," Francesca persisted.

"Okay, what?"

"Where's that book you read to Ethan?"

7

ETHAN AWOKE WITH A start. He'd dozed off while waiting for Brittany to arrive.

He sat for a few moments on the sofa, listening to the ping of rain against the window. It was a relief to wake up now and not feel depression descend like an anvil on his chest. After the accident, all he'd been able to think about was, "Why me?" And then he'd come to realize, "Why not me?"

The first thirty-four years of his life had been charmed. He'd grown up with every advantage. Would it have been more fair for someone much less advantaged to suffer his fate?

He hadn't, however, progressed from depression to acceptance. He refused to learn to use a cane or read braille as long as there was any chance at all that his sight would return.

He supposed what he was at the moment was distracted. Miss Brittany Astor was proving a fine distraction indeed. From force of habit he glanced at his wrist to check the time. Damn.

"Dawson!" he yelled.

He heard Dawson enter the library, the carpet muting the footsteps that had sounded loudly on the unforgiving marble of the foyer.

"What time is it?" Ethan demanded.

"She should be here at any time," Dawson answered, knowing what Ethan was really asking. "Miss Astor rang up earlier to say she'd be bringing your dinner. Is there anything else before I leave for the evening?"

"Did you set out the things we shopped for like I asked you to?"

"Yes, it's all arranged."

"Good. That'll be all, then."

As he heard Dawson let himself out, Ethan decided the apartment was too quiet. Getting up, he made his way slowly to the stereo system where he tried CDs until he found one to his liking. He moved to stand at the window. The rain had stopped.

He smiled. He'd have to remember to beware of an umbrella lurking in the foyer.

One song finished and another began on the rhythm-and-blues CD he'd chosen. He stood at the window waiting while the bawdy sax heightened his anticipation. Tonight music wasn't soothing to the savage beast, it was stirring him.

For the first time he felt blind *and* alive.

BRITTANY HUNG UP the phone and sat staring at the year's publishing schedule on the wall. One of her authors had just called with the equivalent of the "dog ate my homework" excuse about why her manuscript was going to be late. It was a manuscript she'd been counting on, too. She continued to stare at the board as if an answer to the scheduling dilemma would suddenly appear.

To make matters worse, the author had contacted Sandy over a month ago about the possibility of not meeting her deadline and Sandy had assured the writer there would be no problem. And then Sandy had conveniently forgotten to pass the information on to Brittany.

If she weren't in such a good mood, she'd be furious. As it was, she was only annoyed.

Ethan Moss crowded everything from her mind. She was as hooked as any addict, needing the fix of seeing him daily.

And when she wasn't with him she thought about him—the resonance of his voice, the curl of his fair hair on the nape of his neck, the curve of his full bottom lip. . . . She shook her head to clear her thoughts, then spent the last half hour of the day reworking the publishing schedule.

Before arriving at Ethan's apartment she picked up dinner. At first she'd planned to bring Chinese, but she didn't want to risk unintentionally reminding him of what had happened the last time.

She was nervous, uncertain of what his reception would be. Ethan didn't reveal his feelings easily. She supposed being left standing at the altar would do that to a man.

The press had had a field day ten years ago when Ethan's fiancée had stood him up the day of their fancy society wedding. The experience hadn't left him with an aversion to the press; he had shown up in the newspapers frequently. It had apparently left him with an aversion to any kind of serious relationship. He was never pictured with the same woman twice after that.

"I hope that isn't pizza," Ethan called out as she entered the brownstone, the pungent aroma of pizza preceding her.

"Why?" Brittany demanded, taking it to the kitchen.

"I don't like pizza."

"You'll like this."

"What makes you so sure?" he asked, joining her.

"Here, taste," she said, turning to him with a slice of hot pizza in her hand.

Barefoot, he leaned against the butcher-block counter wearing pressed jeans and a navy cashmere V-neck sweater. Unshaven, his hair still damp, he smelled shower fresh and just about took her breath away.

Her hand trembled when she brought the piece of pizza to his lips, coaxing him to taste.

He took a bite and chewed. "Not bad," he said, swallowing. "What kind is it?"

"Cajun shrimp," she answered, feeding him the rest of the slice.

"We need some beer to go with this. Check the fridge. I think we've got some imported stuff in there."

Finding a couple of Heinekens, she opened them. They stood together in the kitchen drinking and eating while listening to the bad advice of a bluesy song on the stereo.

"Napkin," he requested, polishing off the final slice.

She handed him one and he wiped his hands. He set it down and pulled her into his arms when a new piece started. "I hope you can lead," he said, executing a few quick dance steps. "I'm liable to literally dance you off your feet."

She hadn't danced with him since she was fourteen but they fit together perfectly. The song started out fast and jazzy, then turned slow and sensuous. They stood in place, swaying to the music, until the piece ended.

She'd waited—had longed for this moment forever. She'd almost given up hope that it could happen. And now she found herself exactly where she'd always wanted to be—in Ethan's arms.

A low, sexy girlish laugh of pure delight escaped her lips. She was like a little girl who'd gotten Barbie's Dream House for Christmas.

He pulled back at the sound of her laugh, his jaw grazing her cheek.

"Ouch!"

"What'd I do?"

"Whisker burn," she said, rubbing her cheek.

His fingers sought the hurt, rubbing it gently. "Dawson had to leave early. And I can't shave myself. Would you mind terribly...?"

"I don't know. I've never shaved a man before. What if I make a mess of it?"

"I'll chance it. You couldn't be any worse than Dawson. He goes about it as if he were peeling an orange."

"Well, if you think—"

"Come on, let's give it a try," he said, leading the way to the bathroom.

She switched on the light and followed him inside the richly appointed room. The dark wood cabinetry was bathed in a warm glow.

Surveying the dressing table, she realized he'd set her up. Everything was already laid out and waiting for her: plump white towels, a china mug with soap, and a silver-handled brush and matching razor. It all looked very complicated and intimidating.

"Don't you have an electric razor in here somewhere?" Brittany began pulling out drawers to search. No electric razor.

Ethan stilled her hand. "I get razor burn from electric razors."

"Oh."

"I'll teach you," he said, his voice intimating something more than a simple shave. He sat down on the black leather chair in front of the dressing table, his back to the mirror. "First a towel," he instructed.

She reached for the stack of white towels and lifted one to place around his neck. "Don't men shave *before* they shower?" she asked, giving away her inexperience to him.

He didn't comment on the latter, but answered her question. "Hot water and steam soften my beard. You need to soak a washcloth in warm water to wet my face."

She held a washcloth beneath the running water flowing from the gold-plated faucet. Wringing out the cloth, she used it to dampen his face.

"Okay, now the moisturizer. I think it's in a silver canister there."

"Shaving gel?" she asked, picking up a silver flask and reading the label.

"That's it. Put a small amount in your palm and rub it over my face."

She did as he requested, trying to keep her fingers from lingering.

"Now what?" she asked when she was done, wiping her hands on the washcloth and tossing it into the basin.

"You've got to get my face dripping wet. Don't be neat about it."

Using the washcloth, she did as he requested until water splashed onto the towel around his neck.

"Okay, that's good. Now lather up the soap in the mug with the shaving brush, then slather it on my face nice and thick until you've got my whiskers all coated with the stuff."

Brittany added a little water, working the soap in the mug into a billow of lather, then began applying it to his face, careful to cover it evenly. The delicate fragrance of sandalwood scented the air.

"Okay, take the razor and start at my sideburns, making short strokes in the direction my beard grows," he told her.

She picked up the razor, looking at it speculatively. "I don't know. Are you sure about this? What if I slip and nick you?" she asked, not trusting the steadiness of her hands on him. She was pretending a coolness she wasn't certain she could carry off.

"If you nick me, I'll have to fire you," he teased. "And then you won't be able to— Why was it you said you wanted the extra work?"

"I want to buy a cat," she explained, starting to wield the razor as he'd instructed while taking care not to let her hand slip. "I've read that owning a pet is supposed to relieve stress."

"And you're under a lot of stress?"

She was at the moment, she thought, rinsing the razor. "There are a lot of variables in my job. In many ways an editor is only as good as her last book. When an author stumbles, so do I. All sorts of things can go wrong with a book, even if your author gives you a good story."

He indicated she should shave his cheeks next, then continued questioning her about her job. "What sorts of things can go wrong?"

"You're not interested in—"

"No, I am," he assured her. "I suppose in a way I can understand, because backing a play carries risks, too."

"Well, for instance, the cover can go wrong. It can be a gorgeous cover on its own, but fade into the background when it goes on the shelf in the bookstore. Or it can be the subject of the book that kills it. For example, books dealing with the fine arts traditionally don't do well for whatever reason. It can even be something as simple as a snowstorm screwing up distribution of the book, dooming its sales."

She started to shave his chin when she was finished with his cheeks.

"No, save the chin and upper lip for last because that's where my whiskers are the deepest. Do my neck first." He tilted his head back to allow her access, but it didn't work with her standing in front of him.

"Try standing behind me," he suggested.

It worked much better, but only if she rested his head on her chest. She wondered if he could hear her accelerated heartbeat. Feeling weak with desire, she finished shaving him quickly.

"There, all done," she said, laying the razor on the counter, and wiping away the remaining bits of lather with a towel.

"Not quite yet. There should be a balm there to finish up with."

She found it, then smoothed it on with her fingertips until his skin felt soft as a baby's bottom.

"Now, we're done," she announced.

"Tell me something," he said, pulling her onto his lap. "Do you remember your first kiss?"

"Everyone remembers their first kiss," she said, flustered to find herself with her arm around his neck to keep from falling from his lap. She would be sophisticated about this, not act like the giddy fourteen-year-old she was feeling like inside.

"Show me what it was like," he coaxed.

She leaned forward, placing a chaste kiss on his cheek.

"That's it?" Clearly it wasn't what he'd been expecting.

"That's it."

"How old were you?" he asked, laughing.

"I was very grown-up. It was at Miss Cissy's dance recital. I was eight and Ronnie Cresswell was nine. He was very well-mannered—even if he did snicker afterward.

"How about you?" she was surprised to hear herself ask.

"You sure you want to hear?"

She wasn't but she didn't say so.

"Well, as near as I recall, I wasn't very grown-up. I think I was fifteen. It was in a stable. I wasn't very well-mannered, but I didn't snicker afterward. And it went something like this...."

There was no technique. It was all urgent, raw masculinity.

And it was ... he was ... irresistible.

Any defense she might have had against the power of his kiss fell like so many bowling pins in a strike, and with about as much combustive energy.

Her heart did a freefall.

When his lips released hers, they moved along her neck, brushing kisses as he whispered, "Do you know what you've done for me, Brittany? You've made me come to think of myself not as blind, but as blind-fold."

She swallowed dryly, pulling away from his seductive kisses. "Then you've accepted that maybe..."

"No."

"But—"

"I won't. I can't accept it until I have no other choice. There's still a little time—a slight chance that I might see. I have to cling to that. I have to."

Brittany tried to slip from his lap, but he held her there. "Uh-uh. You're not going to leave without telling me a bedtime story."

"I'm fresh out of stories. Your turn."

"But I can't read."

"You don't have to. I made up the second story I told you."

"I know. I didn't hear any pages turning."

"So quit stalling . . ." she said nervously.

"Okay, you're on," he agreed, beginning.

"I'm driving down a dusty Texas road on my way to look at a pony that's for sale. But I've made a wrong turn a long way back. I shoot the gas gauge a nervous glance. It's on the hurting side of Empty. There is nothing but flatland in sight a mile later when it happens—gurgle, glug. I'm out of gas.

"I let my rental car with a broken phone coast to the side of the road, and get out to lean against the fender to wait for the cavalry to arrive. Alas, there's not a horse to be seen.

"An hour later, I'm hot and thirsty, and the horizon is beginning to stack up with clouds. The only thing coming down the road is a gust of wind, twirling a column of dust like a top.

"Just when I'm about to adjust to the idea of

walking for miles in a pair of new shoes to find help, I see it off in the distance—a rusty red pickup truck, the old-fashioned kind with big, rounded fenders. Its clanking is my only reassurance it isn't a mirage.

"The truck slows down as it approaches and comes to a stop alongside my disabled car. It's not the ranch hand I expect, but a rancher's daughter who swings open the cab door, hangs on it and asks, 'Can I give you a hand, mister?'

"'I ran out of gas,' I explain, feeling patently ridiculous.

"'Well, climb on in,' she offers, sliding back behind the wheel of the pickup.

"Grabbing the suit jacket I'd discarded, I climb in alongside her to be rewarded with hot breath and a moist tongue licking my ear.

"'Lizzie, behave,' she orders the black Lab that had been asleep on the seat. The dog lies back down but keeps grinning at me, or so it seems.

"'Where are you heading, mister?' the girl asks me.

"'I was going to see about a pony that's for sale, but I seem to have gotten lost. Do you know anything about the ranch I'm looking for?'

"'Sure do,' she tells me, and a mile or so down

the road she swings the pickup off onto a rutted dirt-and-gravel trail. We ride for a few miles until we come to a clump of trees out in the middle of nowhere. She stops the truck.

"'Why are you stopping here?' I ask as she turns toward me.

"'Looks like it's going to rain,' she answers, just as fat droplets begin to hit the windshield.

"'Looks like you're right,' I agree, uncertain what the weather has to do with anything.

"She then proceeds to prop her feet up on the dashboard, splaying her legs a provocative distance apart. Her jean cutoffs only emphasize their tanned attractiveness. The red high-top sneakers and white slouch socks on her feet accentuate her trim ankles.

"Her dog has lost interest in me and is asleep on the floor of the pickup.

"I'm wide-awake as the girl reaches to unbuckle my suit pants.

"I ask her what's going on—not that I mind. I just want to be clear about it.

"She smiles, pleased and confident in her ability to seduce me. And then she says, 'I'm doing as I promised. I'm going to give you a hand. Unless, of course . . .' She hesitates.

"'Of course...' I repeat, waiting for her to lead me.

"'Well, it's just that I love to make love naked in the back of my pickup truck when it rains. It's so sensual, don't you think?'

"'Why don't I tell you in a few minutes?' I reply.

"She laughs, unzipping me. Reaching inside my pants to find me, she surrounds me with her fingers, squeezing, encouraging. 'Mister, I sure hope we're talking more than a few minutes, or I'll have to think about letting you walk the rest of the way.'

"With that, she grabs the blanket covering the seat and hops out of the cab, heading for the back of the pickup. She spreads the blanket out, the denim fringe of her cutoffs framing the curves of her cheeks as she leans against the lowered tailgate.

"The rain begins to increase in intensity as she turns to me and unbuttons my shirt. I return the favor, then hop out of my pants while she kicks off her cutoffs.

"She is a vision in nothing but her red canvas high-tops. Smiling with wicked intent, she grabs hold of the only article of clothing I'm still wearing.

"'Come here, mister,' she orders, tugging me toward her by my loosened tie.

"As I cover her body with mine in the back of the pickup truck, the sky opens up. Water sluices down our bodies as we begin a session of heated, passionate lovemaking.

"Wet and slippery, our bodies slide against each other. We are locked together intimately. Control slips away. Convention slips away.

"Your nails dig into my back as the rain continues and you cry out my name.

"Ignoring your pleas for completion, I continue to do wickedly sensual things to you, torturing you with teasing. . . brushing. . . lifting . . . smoothing . . . caressing.

"You plead for harder, pointing your toes and arching your soft pink body against my tanned hard one.

"I make you coax me until you are squirming and moaning beneath me with your hands on my hips, your head moving from side to side, taut and straining.

"You're reduced to making wild little whimpering sounds as I move my mouth to make yours my captive. Sexual hunger claws at you while I deepen the kiss, my mouth silencing your begging, your ragged breathing.

"And then I fill you, thrusting as we hurl into ecstasy.

"The rain continues, warm and hard. You laugh as I lie spent beside you, counting the adorable freckles on your nose."

8

BRITTANY SLAPPED her hand to her nose.

"Wait a minute! How do you know I have freckles?" she demanded. She tried to slip from his lap, but he wasn't having any of it.

"I wasn't talking about you. It was a fantasy, remember? You asked me to make up a story. It was the first thing that came into my mind. It was make-believe, Brittany."

"You may have started out using just your imagination, but you really got into it at the end. You went from the euphemistic *she* to *me*."

She waved her hand in front of his eyes. "You can see, can't you?" she accused.

"No. Not a thing. Not a *damn* thing."

"If you can't see anything, then how do you know I've got freckles on my nose?"

"*Have* you?" he asked, playing with her, not taking her at all seriously.

"You know I do." She took his chin in her hand. "What I want to know is how you came to know about my having freckles."

"Dawson told me?" he ventured lamely.

"Try again."

"Okay. You've got me dead to rights. I know you have freckles because I remember seeing them."

He remembered her! "When? At my coming-out party?"

"That must have been it."

"I don't understand. Why didn't you say anything when I applied for the job?"

"Because it didn't matter to me if the person I hired to read to me had freckles," he cajoled with a laugh.

"But—"

He silenced her curiosity with a kiss that demonstrated all the technique he'd learned since he'd been fifteen. It was certainly an impressive amount.

She hadn't stood a chance. She was melting in his embrace—long before his tongue fought past her inhibitions to slip inside her mouth, its thrust sure and erotic.

"What—what was that all about?" Brittany asked, when he ended the kiss. She desperately wanted to be more than an amusing diversion.

"I just wanted to show you I'm an equal-opportunity voyeur. As it happens, I like both my fantasy women *and* my real women with freckles."

"Tricia Edwards didn't have one freckle," Brittany muttered, still jealous of the beautiful woman Ethan had almost married.

The teasing note was gone from his voice at the mention of Tricia's name. "How do you know so much about Tricia?"

"I must have seen her with you," Brittany answered. In truth, Brittany had kept a close eye on Tricia throughout the entire courtship.

At first she'd tried to imitate Tricia. When it had become patently clear that was an impossible task, she had tried to believe that he would tire of her, come to his senses. The announcement of Tricia and Ethan's engagement had put the lie to that fantasy.

Francesca had read the announcement aloud at the breakfast table. Brittany had been eating orange marmalade.

She hadn't eaten marmalade since.

While she'd done her best to hide her shock—which hadn't been all that difficult, as Francesca was bubbling over with news about a new beau she'd met—Brittany had had to face reality.

Ethan was going to marry Tricia.

"Well, you certainly didn't meet Tricia at our wedding," Ethan muttered.

"Were you—"

"I don't want to talk about it," he said, cutting her off.

But she did. She wanted to know if he was still in love with Tricia. Was that why he'd never married? Was that the real reason he didn't want to talk about what had happened?

Brittany knew she wouldn't get anywhere by trying to force the issue. Ethan would have to want to talk about it himself. He would have to be the one to bring up any discussion, as it was apparently still an emotionally painful subject. For now, discussion of the fiancée who'd jilted him at the altar on the day of their wedding was forbidden.

She made an effort to slip from his lap again. "I think maybe I should be going."

"I disagree. I think maybe you should be staying." The sexy invitation in his voice brought back the romantic mood she had broken with the mention of Tricia's name.

"I don't know . . ." What if what she suspected was true? What if he was still in love with Tricia? She'd be setting herself up for heartbreak. But then, if she passed up this opportunity to have Ethan make love to her and the chance never came again, she'd never forgive herself.

Was it true, as she'd read, that it was better to regret the things you'd done, than to regret what you hadn't done?

"If you want to leave, I understand," Ethan said, interrupting her thoughts, a note of resigned acceptance in his voice.

"You do?"

"You feel sorry for me and you enjoy flirting with me because you think of me as being safe. You won't get involved with me."

"You're wrong, Ethan."

"Am I?"

Maybe it was something she'd always regret, but she would stay. "I'd like to stay."

"Do you know what you're saying?"

"Yes. I know."

"No more games, Brittany. I want you. I want you in my bed."

"How conventional of you. Sure you wouldn't prefer the back of a pickup truck?"

"Not in the middle of New York City," he said, his wicked laugh acknowledging the fantasy.

"This bed, where is it?" Brittany asked.

Ethan stood, still holding her in his arms. "Why don't I just show you," he suggested, carrying her from the bathroom and down the hall, then up the stairs.

The walls of the master bedroom were blue, the floors were bleached wood and the iron bed was curtained in Fortuny white silk, Brittany saw after Ethan had put her down and she'd turned on the light.

Brittany let out a low whistle, and almost felt a bridelike blush.

"What?" Ethan asked.

"That's some bed to be deflowered upon—"

"Deflowered? You aren't a—"

"No. Not actually. But in a way. It's been a long time.... My first time wasn't..."

"Wasn't what?" he asked, concern etching his voice.

What was she going to tell him? Certainly not the truth. The truth was that she'd made love to a man she hadn't been in love with. A man whose only fault had been that he wasn't Ethan. She couldn't tell him that. She couldn't tell him that she'd been celibate for years. He'd think she was a twit, wouldn't he?

"It wasn't as special as I'd thought it would be," she finally answered, giving him part, but not all of the truth.

"Then I'd better get it right, hadn't I?" He said it without a shade of doubt that he would... could. Maybe that was what this was all about for him—sex with her as a way for him to reassure himself he could still do some things as well as he always had.

He sat down on the bed. "I'd like you to undress for me. Take your time, I want to listen."

A tiny shiver traversed her spine at the sensual candor he'd displayed with his request. First she stepped out of her shoes, kicking them aside to skitter on the hardwood floor. Then she unbuttoned her double-breasted coatdress. She smiled, realizing its navy color matched Ethan's sweater. She didn't know why it pleased her, it just did.

She laid the dress across a nearby chair as it had suddenly occurred to her that she had to go to work in the morning. And even though the thought of wearing the same dress to work for two days running and its damning implications gave her pause, there was no way she would allow doubt to enter her mind. Like Scarlett, she'd think about that tomorrow.

She removed her tights from beneath her slip, then crossed arms to raise the garment over her head with a fluid swish. Dropping it to the floor beside her discarded tights, she went to Ethan.

She felt like a kid at Christmas.

She could not quite believe her good fortune at finding herself alone with the object of her desire; a most special present to unwrap.

The dream had become a reality.

He pulled her down onto the bed beside him.

"Let me help you with this," she said, tugging his sweater over his head, yearning to feel the warmth of his skin on hers.

His lazy grin should have told her that he was ready to accelerate the pace. He turned her onto her back beneath him so that they were stretched out crosswise on the plush bed. She'd meant to keep her eyes open to record every moment, but her eyelids grew heavy as she succumbed to his drugging kisses.

His hands threaded through her hair to hold her captive while he feathered caresses down her cheek. Groaning, he kissed her chin openmouthed and sucking.

"You smell like a warm summer rain, freckle face. Is that possible?"

Brittany laughed softly. "Well, I wasn't going to tell you, but since you noticed...I'm wearing a body talc called Spring Rain. Probably your fantasy wasn't as out-of-the-blue as you imagined."

"So inspire me some more, freckle face."

"I just might if you call me Brittany," she coaxed, nibbling his ear, then kissing the corners of his mouth. She sucked his bottom lip, biting it playfully.

"Umm, I think I've forgotten my own name, freckle face," he murmured sensually, as she continued her assault on his mouth.

"Brittany," she repeated. "My name is Brittany, not freckle face. Come on, put your lips together. You can say it."

"Umm . . . but I don't want to put my lips together," he replied, letting her tongue into his mouth.

She made him cry uncle, her passion making up for any lack of expertise.

"Brittany, love," he breathed.

"Good boy!"

"I don't think I've ever been called that before," he said, chuckling.

She began kissing his fingers, sucking them; then she licked his palm.

"Bad girl!"

"I don't think I've ever been called that before."

"Well, we'll just have to see what we can do about corrupting you a bit then, won't we?"

"We? Is there a mouse in your pocket?" she asked, laughing.

"Why don't you check?"

Picking up the bait, she slipped her hand between them. "Nope, no mouse."

"Are you sure? Maybe you haven't searched hard enough. Maybe—"

"I've searched as thoroughly as I can with you on top of me—"

"Oh, is that a problem?" He levered himself off her and rolled onto his back. Folding his hands behind his head, he offered, "Have at it, freckle face."

"Brittany, it's Brittany," she muttered, accepting his challenge nonetheless.

She ran her hands over the wide expanse of his muscular chest, flicking his small brown nipples with her tongue, and then moving lower, trailing baby kisses to his navel. Narrow-hipped as he was, his jeans had slipped to ride suggestively low. She continued her delicious torture, raking her teeth along his waistband.

"Nice, very nice . . ." Brittany murmured a little while later.

At that, Ethan maneuvered himself above Brittany again. "Time for *you* to show and tell." He unsnapped the front closure of her satin bra, freeing her to his touch.

Squeezing her breasts gently, he singsonged, "'And these are a few of my favorite things....' Tell me, are they dusted with fairy dust, too?"

"What?"

"You know, freckles," he answered, closing his mouth over one, alternately sucking and licking it.

"No. No freckles anywhere on my body except my nose." And for the first time she was almost sorry about that. It was his way of putting it—"fairy dust." He could be quite lovely, but then she'd instinctively known that. He'd been very kind to her at her debut. He'd mumbled something about always liking to dance with the prettiest girl before he left. She'd assumed he said it to all the girls.

She'd wistfully hoped that he hadn't.

"Describe your breasts to me," he coaxed, taking them into his warm hands.

"I'm not going—"

"Come on, humor me, freckle face. I'm at a bit of a disadvantage here. After all, you've 'met' all of me now, haven't you?"

"Well..." When he put it like that, how could she possibly refuse him? She thought for a moment and then said hopefully, "They're sort of pale and ... pretty...."

His hands cosseted them playfully. "And perky. You forgot perky."

What did a girl say to that? Not knowing at all, she just smiled. Happily.

"I've got a deal for you," he said, levering himself to his side. "If you help me take off my jeans, I'll help you take off your panties."

"You're too kind, sir."

As he lay back on his back, she tugged his jeans down his legs.

"I know. It's a failing of mine," he agreed, lifting his hips to assist her in removing his jeans the rest of the way.

He rubbed his hands together. "Now it's my turn. What's your pleasure? Shall I slip them off slowly with kisses? Or would you prefer I ravish you by ripping them from your body?"

"Oh. Well, I think ravishment is out. I have to go to work in the morning."

"Oh, and I was so hoping for ravishing. Are you quite sure I can't talk you into—" He began slipping his finger beneath her panties and his tongue in her ear.

Two minutes later she voted for ravishment.

It was a very popular vote.

And a very rewarding one.

"So introduce me," he said wickedly, moving her hands to her sex.

"I can't—"

"Gotcha, freckle face. You forgot I can't see, didn't you. Well, to tell you the truth I almost did, too. You're making me see the most marvelous mind pictures."

Her eyes, which had drifted closed in shy embarrassment, flew open.

"Which means you're going to have to give me a hand, so to speak," he said, waiting.

She swallowed dryly, looking at his penis seemingly straining toward her as if it were magnetized.

"Look, I don't want to rush you, but I feel I ought to warn you I'm so hot, the party might be over before it starts, if it doesn't start soon."

She didn't think it was time to mention she'd sent out the party invitation years ago and he was the one who was late. But he was right. Much as she'd like the night to last forever, she was also anxious to feel him inside her.

He drew a sharp intake of breath when she took him in hand to guide him.

"Careful . . ." he said, as if she were handling nitroglycerin.

He slid into her as smooth as satin. Again and again.

He'd lied to her.

There wasn't any way he was going to party without her. Each thrust was slow and sure . . . coaxing, demanding, until small tremors started up her thighs and soft moans escaped her lips.

And then he was off, his thrust quicker as she clenched around him, exploding in passionate spasms.

He relinquished the tight rein of control he'd held until she was satisfied.

Her pleasure seemed to be the applause he needed. With one deep thrust he came, crying out her name . . ."Brittany."

BRITTANY SAT IN THE middle of her living room floor surrounded by her scrapbooks.

She had left Ethan's apartment at seven, planning on going in to work. But it had been impossible. It was bad enough that she would have shown up for work in the same dress for two days in a row—something her assistant would never let pass without comment. The deal breaker was the fact that she was wearing a pair of Ethan's boxer shorts under it. She had "borrowed" them while he was still asleep.

Her mood had shifted back and forth like a pendulum between joy, despair and hysteria during the cab ride to her office. When they'd arrived at her office building, she'd panicked and given the cabbie the address of her apartment, deciding she'd call in sick for the day.

It had been an irresponsible thing to do.

But so had making love with Ethan last night.

Flipping the page of the scrapbook on her lap, she looked down at the newspaper clipping with Ethan's photo. It had been taken during an exciting final match at Smith's Lawn. Ethan's team had narrowly beaten the opposing players. Ethan's pony, Riley, had been voted best-playing pony, and a sweaty, jubilant Ethan held up the prize.

As she looked at the picture she thought back over what had happened between them last night. She had been very foolish for a lot of reasons. Not using protection was inexcusable. So, too, was taking advantage of Ethan's blindness. He was in an emotionally fragile state. If he had used her, at least *he* had an excuse.

Hearing the key turn in the lock on the apartment door, Brittany looked up.

"So you finally came home," Francesca chastised with mock disfavor as she stepped into the room. "Wait a minute, aren't you supposed to be at the office?"

"Yes, *mom*. And where have you been? Are you just getting home from yesterday's photo shoot?"

"I was out getting a manicure, baby sister. And *I* was home all night last night." She tossed down her purse and waited.

"I spent the night with Ethan," Brittany admitted in a breathy rush.

"And . . . ?" Francesca's attention was rapt, her curiosity nearly palpable as she came closer in order to hear every delicious detail.

"Francesca!" Brittany shook her head and turned the page of the scrapbook, studying a picture of Ethan dressed in a tuxedo on the opening night of a Broadway play he'd helped finance. He was standing beneath the marquee, smiling with the flush of a firstnight success. The play had gone on to be a longrunning hit.

"It just sort of happened."

"Uh-huh . . ."

"It did," Brittany insisted. "Don't make it sound so calculated. It wasn't like that."

"So what was it like? Did it live up to your expectations after all these years of dreaming about Ethan? Was he as wonderful between the sheets as the gossip columns would have us believe?"

"We, ah, didn't actually make it between the sheets," Brittany answered, finding herself actually blushing. "It was fine, okay? I don't want to talk about it."

"Oh, no, you don't." Francesca lifted the scrapbook from Brittany's lap and set it on the coffee table. "Come sit here beside me and give me every sexy detail. I told you all about my beaus. You owe me. I even told you about what Lance Bergen did, senior year."

"No, you didn't." Brittany pulled up her socks, smiling. Ethan had certainly "rolled down her socks" last night. "I read about Lance in your diary."

"You always were a big reader, weren't you? I suppose you were destined to be an editor even then."

Brittany joined her sister on the chintz sofa. Brittany had changed into a T-shirt and still wore Ethan's boxers. She tucked her legs beneath her. "Okay, Francesca, I suppose I do owe you for reading your diary. Ethan was... I never knew it could be like that."

"That's because you're in love with him, baby sister. It makes all the difference in the world."

"But what if— Oh, I'm so afraid last night was a mistake," Brittany blurted out. "What if it was just Ethan proving to himself that he could still function in one area of his life?"

"But I thought he was doing okay. Didn't you tell me the two of you went out shopping and to see a Broadway show one night?"

"That's true," Brittany admitted.

"So maybe you're worried about nothing. Maybe Ethan is as smitten with you, as you are with him."

"Oh, Francesca, wouldn't that be wonderful? But what if . . . what if he finds out what I did? He'd never speak to me again."

"Well, you'll just have to make sure he never finds out. That ought to be easy enough. The only ones who know about it are you and me—and I'm certainly not going to tell him about it."

Brittany didn't want to think about it. Didn't want to think of anything that would spoil the fantasy that Ethan was smitten with her. So she changed the subject. "You haven't said how your shoot for *Rolling Stone* went yesterday."

"Oh, yeah, I almost forgot to tell you!" Francesca said, her eyes bright with excitement. "You'll never guess. Tucker and I got the cover. Can you believe it?"

"That's fantastic. When does it come out?"

"I'm not sure. My agency is supposed to let me know. And I've got more news. The agency called this morning and they're faxing my portfolio to the director of Tucker Gable's new music video. Tucker requested me."

"So he liked you, huh?" Brittany teased.

"Well, maybe I flirted just a little. He's so hot in that black leather vest he wears. And he's got those honed biceps to die for."

"So maybe I'll be getting a rock star for a brother-in-law, then," Brittany continued teasing.

"Bite your tongue. I won't be 'the model and the rock star'—pu-leeze!"

"I thought you said he was hot."

"*I* was hot—and it's all your fault. You were the one who lent me that book you read to Ethan. Mercy."

"Let's see," Brittany said, pretending to write in the air. "Mrs. Francesca Gable . . ."

"Mrs. Brittany Moss . . ." Francesca countered.

And then they both collapsed in giggles against each other.

ETHAN ROLLED OVER and reached for Brittany. His grasp came up empty. He felt around on the bed.

Nothing.

She was gone.

It *had* happened, hadn't it? He hadn't dreamed it, had he?

Just like he'd dreamed that he could see again.

Of course, he couldn't see. He'd found that out when he woke up just seconds ago.

Disappointment washed over him. He'd so wanted to wake up and *see Brittany* in his bed beside him.

He supposed that either was too much to hope for.

9

CALLING IN SICK had been a mistake.

She was being made to pay for her lie simply by working to catch up. This Wednesday felt more like a Monday.

She glanced at her watch. It was three-thirty and her assistant wasn't back from lunch yet. Sandy was taking advantage of the situation.

Brittany had inherited Sandy from the editor who'd held the position before her. Sandy had believed the job would be hers, and resented Brittany's getting it. Sandy was being ridiculous: assistants didn't move into senior editor jobs.

But Sandy, with the trust fund, was used to getting everything she wanted, when she wanted it.

She couldn't imagine Sandy waiting ten years for a man, as she had for Ethan. No. When Sandy was ready for a man, she would probably just call up Lord & Taylor and order one on the charge account that Daddy paid.

The phone rang in the outer office.

Since her assistant wasn't there to answer it, Brittany picked it up. It was the agent conducting the auction they were bidding in with two other publishing houses. It was Brittany's turn in the final round.

She had to pull everyone involved in the decision-making process out of meetings because they couldn't afford to miss this negotiation.

In the end they wound up passing on the book. The consensus was that while the book was very good, the author was more trouble than she was worth. No one wanted to work with her. And since Triple Knight had a lot of inventory, they decided not to tie up that much money with what could be a real problem project.

Sandy finally got back from lunch with the West Coast agent who'd dropped in unexpectedly. Brittany couldn't complain. She'd sent Sandy off with her because she hadn't had the time to do lunch with the woman herself.

After exchanging some business news, the agent left and Brittany locked herself in her office to write her speech for the sales conference. She didn't get much speech writing done, however. All she could think about was Ethan—about the way his abdomen tightened when she'd kissed him "there"; about the way he looked after sex . . . so carefree.

She'd called Dawson on Tuesday and told him to tell Ethan she had to work Tuesday night, so she hadn't seen Ethan last night. But she would tonight.

Her pen slashed out the lines of copy she'd written. She balled the paper up and tossed it in the trash.

She was going to duck out early. Maybe buy something new to wear. She was feeling both excited and anxious about seeing Ethan in a few hours.

How would he feel about her now that he'd had some time to think about it?

Brittany glanced at the clock as she gathered up her things. It was only four-thirty. Closing her office door behind her, she called out to Sandy, who was on the phone, "I'm leaving for the day."

Sandy covered the mouthpiece on her phone. "But it's—" she started to object.

"See you in the morning," Brittany said, with a careless wave. She was enjoying being bad.

"Is THAT ALL THE MAIL then?" Ethan asked, sipping a glass of Chardonnay to relax.

"Yes, the invitation I just read you was the final piece of mail," Dawson replied.

"Good. Answer the other pieces as we discussed, if you would, and leave the invitation you just read to me on the desk."

"I'm going to the stables, Ethan. Would you like to come along? Riley would be happy to see you."

"Not today, Dawson. But soon," he promised, as Dawson left the library.

Ethan was nervous. He took another sip of wine.

Had Brittany really had to work late last night? Or was she having second thoughts about what had happened between them? He really hoped not. He desperately hoped not.

He certainly wasn't.

Hiring Brittany was the smartest move he'd ever made in his life. She had challenged him, and made him see for the first time that in a worst-case scenario he could live a fulfilling life even without his sight.

Brittany's imagination and spirit had inspired him. She'd refused to accept his melancholy. She'd dragged him kicking and screaming into the possibilities.

Her flirtation had charmed him. He'd been a more than willing partner in their dance of seduction. And last night had been like nothing he'd ever felt before. Talking with a woman in bed, laughing with a woman in bed.

Trusting a woman—something he'd never thought he'd do again.

WHEN BRITTANY ENTERED her apartment she was assaulted by music, music so loud it bounced off the walls.

"What's going on?" she yelled to Francesca.

Francesca jumped up and pulled her in front of the television. "You've got to see this. It's the best pelvis since Elvis. Would you look at Dwight Yoakam get down? He must put those jeans on wet."

Brittany didn't answer. Instead, she stared at the images of the music video on the television. The guy had charisma, no doubt about it. Charisma and jeans were an unbeatable combination.

The video ended and Francesca turned down the sound so they could talk.

"Is that what you've been doing all day?" Brittany asked. "And if so, where do I apply for the same job? I've had the world's worst day."

"But you're home early."

"I fled."

"What happened?"

"What didn't? Don't ask," Brittany said, holding up her hands, palms out. "Tell me your day instead. It had to be better than mine. And tell me you have something great I can borrow to wear tonight to see Ethan. I was too bummed out even to stop and shop on the way home. I just set the tractor beam on this building and zoned out."

"Oh, poor baby. Well, let's see what I have in my closet. I think I've got a new Azzedine Alaïa."

"Forget it, I'm not wearing one of those dresses," Brittany assured her.

"Why not? You've got a great shape."

"Yeah, right. To wear an Azzedine Alaïa you can't have eaten a french fry within the past year. Let me see what else you have. You haven't said how your day went, or did you spend it in front of the television trying to find Tucker Gable videos?"

"No. Well, at least not all of the day. I checked with my booker this morning while I had a bagel with cream cheese and juice. See, I do eat," Francesca declared, making a face at Brittany. "I had a 'go-see' to show my book at eleven and the client put me on hold for first option. I left my composite with them and I came home to watch music videos on television just in case I do get a shot at the part in Tucker's video. I want to know what I'm trying out for."

"What about Chelsea Stone? I thought she always did Tucker's music videos with him," Brittany said, considering a short black dress and then passing on it, continuing to rifle through Francesca's closet.

"Chelsea married Dakota Law, remember. And now she's nine-and-a-half-months pregnant or something. So Tucker's hiring a model to play the love interest in the video because the first single from his new album is a love song."

"So, do you think you can fake being attracted to Tucker Gable, him being a rock star and all . . . ?" Brittany teased.

"Do you want to borrow my clothes, or not?"

"Sorry. Not another word about Tucker Gable will cross my lips," Brittany promised, selecting the short black dress after all. "Okay, accessory queen, do your thing," Brittany said, holding the dress up to herself.

"All right, but remember I plan my outfits around my shoes."

Brittany groaned. Francesca was probably talking about thigh-high suede boots.

"What would you think if I told you I'm toying with the idea of taking acting classes?" Francesca asked, searching through boxes of shoes for just the right pair.

"You mean because you turned twenty-eight? I wish you'd quit obsessing about your age. Even Calvin Klein used one of his original models this year. Modeling isn't the youth-obsessed career it once was."

"That's true enough. But I've got this feeling I'm going to need a new career, anyway. Computer technology isn't far from creating the images now done with photography. Just think of the cut in cost. And reducing models' fees is very much in the news. I don't know, maybe you've got the right idea, after all, Brittany. Maybe we should just get a cat. We can be spinster sisters, sharing an apartment with our cats," Francesca said, coming up at last with a pair of impossibly sexy black pumps styled with satin ribbon crisscrossed in front.

"Great. You can come shopping with me next week for the cat I've been wanting."

"I was kidding, Brittany. Here, take the shoes, and add my Chrome Heart jewelry. Ethan will be on his knees by morning."

"Francesca!"

"Oh, please. You're the one who stayed out all night, not me."

Brittany wondered if Ethan was spending his day remembering. Wondered if he was smiling at the oddest times like she was. Wondered if she was letting her hopes and dreams fly too high like a hot-air balloon that would come crashing back to earth.

No, she couldn't be wrong about what they'd shared.

Not now. Not after all this time.

"What are you daydreaming about?" Francesca asked.

"I was thinking that you'll have to corrupt Tucker Gable, big sister," Brittany improvised and ducked away from the sneaker Francesca threw at her.

"You've got to be kidding. Tucker's more likely to corrupt me out of my job. The man eats nothing but junk food. He went through a half-dozen jelly doughnuts on the shoot. I'm clueless about how the man stays so lean and mean."

"Maybe if you ask him real nice, like, he might show you."

"Well, it's not nervous energy he's burning. He's the most laid-back person I think I've ever met. I think he could sleep through a plane crash."

"Maybe it's all that sex and rock and roll. I understand making love burns up about three hundred calories. Just holding the guitar pick probably burns up—oh, I don't know, say an extra fifty."

"Brittany!"

"Well, I owed you for that crack you made about me being a spinster with a cat."

"Meow."

"YOU'RE LATE," Ethan said when Brittany entered the library to join him.

"I had a terrible day at the office."

"I was afraid you'd decided not to come back."

"Why?"

Ethan shrugged. "You could have had second thoughts. Decided it wasn't a good idea. Decided it wasn't what you wanted, after all. It's not like I haven't had any experience with a woman changing her mind." His last words were said under his breath, but Brittany heard them.

"I stayed with you because I wanted to," she told him. "And I came here tonight because I wanted to."

"Come here and show me how much...."

She went to join him on the sofa, settling into the comfort of his embrace.

"So tell me about your terrible day," he said. "And when did you start wearing short sexy dresses to the office?"

"How do you—"

"I copped a feel."

"I thought if I dressed up tonight I'd feel better."

"Believe me when I tell you you couldn't feel any better to me. So tell me about your terrible, rotten, no-good day."

"Trust me, Ethan, you really don't want to hear about my day. Let's talk about something much more interesting. Say, for example, why you whistle after sex."

"Yes, I do want to hear about your day. I'd like to know what an editor's day is like. Don't you have a cushy job where all you do all day is sit and read books?"

"Okay, you asked for it. I'm in a meeting this morning and my book gets bumped up on the list."

"That's good, isn't it?" Ethan asked, nibbling on her earlobe.

"Yes, that's good. But because my book was bumped up on the list, I've got to write more catalog copy for it since my book will now take up a whole page in that month's catalog."

"So did you get the copy written?" he asked, kissing her neck.

"Not before my boss, the executive editor, summons me to tell me she needs me to get her an overnight promotional quote on another book."

"Not good, huh?"

"It gets better. I have to get the quote from a big-name author who not only hasn't read the book, but who doesn't have time to read the book because she's on deadline for her own book."

"Is it time for lunch yet?" he asked sympathetically.

"Lunch? Today there was no lunch. My assistant had lunch. She had a *three-hour* lunch with a West Coast agent who happened to drop in unannounced to see me about one of her clients. Since I was also involved in an auction for a book my publisher wanted to acquire and couldn't leave, I sent my assistant to lunch with the agent on the company tab. And my assistant didn't even bring back a breadstick."

"Did you fire her?"

"I'm hopeless—I couldn't fire a serial killer."

"She's not—"

"No, of course not. She's harmless. Except she wants my job. Though now that I think of it, I can't imagine why anyone would. Where was I? Oh, it was time for a strategy meeting, which I was pulled out of ten minutes later because it was my turn to bid in the auction. The agent conducting the auction tells me the bid is up to $50,000 and I have to gather all the pertinent people together to see if we want to match or raise it."

"Come here, stretch out on the sofa. Put your head in my lap and relax."

"That's what all the boys say."

"So the answer is no?"

"You do have a pretty irresistible lap. . . ."

"So, your terrible, rotten, no-good day is over. You deserve a treat."

"*Who* deserves a treat? And my day isn't over. I still have to work on my speeches for the sales conference. I diligently promised myself that I wasn't going to write it at the last minute like I always do."

Brittany knew she was rattling on. But she couldn't seem to stop herself. She was by turns nervous, excited and afraid.

It was hard having a chance at getting what she'd always dreamed of having. So much could go wrong. And then she'd have nothing at all. Not even her dream.

"No more work today," Ethan insisted. "I have a surprise for you."

"In your lap?" Brittany groaned inwardly, not believing what she'd blurted out.

Ethan laughed. "Maybe later. But for now I had Dawson order something sent over from Houghtaling's Mousse Pie Ltd. Do you think you could manage a bite of truffle pie?"

The trouble was, the delicious chocolate-espresso flavor Ethan had ordered didn't exactly calm her down. With no coaxing at all she was in his lap after dessert. With even less coaxing, she was engaged in heavy petting.

"Hold that thought," Ethan said, coming up for air.

"Where are you going?" Brittany asked, as he shifted her from his lap and rose from the sofa.

"I need to do a couple of things. First, I need to put away the rest of the pie. Maybe if Dawson has a piece in the morning, it will improve his mood. And second, and more important, I need to get some protection."

"Oh." Brittany was embarrassed that he'd had to be the one to think of it. He really did kiss her senseless.

"I think you ought to know in case you were worried about it, they did a lot of blood work on me when I had the accident. I'm safe."

"And, ah, so am I, because...ah, well, there hasn't been..."

"And I'm glad," he said, bending down to kiss her. "Why don't you put on some mood music while I take care of things."

Ethan felt his way to the kitchen, while Brittany went to look through the collection of CDs next to the stereo. She didn't see Dwight Yoakam's latest release, so instead chose a CD of chamber music. She needed to chill. Take it slow and easy. Collect her wits about her.

"What is that?" Ethan asked, rejoining her in the library a few moments later.

"I don't know. One of your CDs."

"It's not one of mine. It must belong to the owner of the brownstone."

"Do you want me to put on something else?" she asked, returning to the stereo to look again through the CDs.

He came up behind her, nuzzling her neck, his hands on her hips pressing her back against him. "I was thinking more along the lines of you taking something off," he whispered hoarsely, turning her into his arms to dance.

"I've been thinking of nothing else all day. I was so distracted, Dawson finally gave up in frustration before we'd finished answering the mail."

"Umm . . . you're good on your feet," she murmured, as he did a smooth fancy step.

"I'm even better off them," he promised, pulling her close and spinning them, his lips on hers in a slow, eating kiss that had her weak with desire.

"You're not playing fair," she said, dizzy.

"I warned you about that, didn't I?"

He had. But she hadn't listened. Hadn't wanted to hear anything that would make her think twice about what she was doing. About wading into dangerous emotional waters. It was time to finally know if her love for Ethan would sink or swim.

"What are you thinking about?" she asked, after they'd danced in silence for a while.

"I was wondering if you'd— Oh, never mind."

"What?"

"When I was sitting at my desk today, thinking about us, I had this wicked thought...."

Brittany didn't hear anything he said past the word *us*. Her heart beat rapidly with excitement.

"I told you it was wicked...."

"What? What were you saying?" Brittany asked, realizing he'd asked her something.

"I was wondering if you'd agree to having sex on my desk. Then, whenever I'm sitting there, I could remember us."

"Ethan, you have way too much free time."

"Tell me about it."

She hadn't meant to hurt his feelings, to bring up his being sightless. "I'll agree to do it on one condition," she hurriedly said, trying to make up for her carelessness. "I get to clear it off first. I don't fancy being stapled or anything."

"Be my guest," Ethan said eagerly.

Brittany went to his desk and began gathering up the papers and books on top of it. As she was moving the silver water pitcher, a formal invitation caught her eye. She picked it up.

"What's this for? Don't tell me you're still going to debutante balls," she said, waving the invitation in the air.

"Is that the invitation to my class reunion? If it is, just toss it. I'm not going to attend."

"Why not?"

"I think that should be obvious. I have no stomach for going and having my old classmates feel sorry for the blind guy. I don't want anyone's pity."

"That isn't how it sounds."

"What do you mean?"

She was probably being way out of line, but someone had to tell him. Dawson more or less ignored him, and his family coddled him.

"People take their signals on how to treat you from the way you behave. If you hide from the world instead of going out and living your life to the best of your ability, on your own terms, then, yes, people are going to feel sorry for you."

"Will you go with me?"

"If you'd like."

"I'd like."

She could tell by the way he said it that he would. Maybe that was why the invitation had been lying all by itself on the desk where she couldn't possibly miss seeing it. He'd wanted to ask her, but had been hesitant for whatever reason a prideful man might have.

He made his way across the room toward her.

"I hope the desk is cleared off. If it isn't, I may do it in one fell swoop," he said, leaning her back across it.

And then the game they'd been playing since she'd brought along that book to read, resumed. Ethan picked up and embellished one of her stories, his voice laced with passion.

"So, young lady, do you understand why you've been sent to the dean's office? Do you understand that I can expel you for your misconduct in class?"

Brittany became a willing participant in this new twist....

"But Dean, isn't there any way I can get back into my classes? Surely there must be some extra project I could do for you as penance. I promise I'll be really, really good. It could be our little secret. You wouldn't have to report me that way."

"Well, young lady, as it happens, I could use an assistant for, say, a half hour every day...."

Ethan's hand began inching up Brittany's sexy, short black dress.

"Oh my, Dean. Does this mean I have a chance at a 4.0 grade average?"

"Well, young lady, we'll have to see. To get a perfect grade point average, you'll have to be really, really good."

Twenty minutes later, Brittany smiled with delight at the sound of Ethan's carefree whistle.

10

ETHAN STOOD AT THE window in the library.

He was alone, having sent Dawson out on a morning of errands.

The library had become Ethan's safe place almost as soon as he'd moved into the rented brownstone. It was as if he were a bear and the library was his den. How fitting, then, that he should "wake up" from what had been a very long hibernation, in this very room. It had happened suddenly—last night, when he'd been dancing with Brittany.

It had been when he'd spun them around very quickly.

Brittany hadn't noticed anything because he'd tried his best not to let on. At first he almost hadn't believed it himself when he saw the shadowy images before his eyes. It had been like walking into bright sunlight from a darkened movie theater.

Brittany hadn't spent the night because of an early meeting.

He'd stayed up the rest of the night, afraid that if he went to sleep, he would wake up sightless again. He'd tried watching Letterman before he realized he might be straining his eyes, damaging them.

The doctors had explained all about the bruised retinas, hemorrhaging, et cetera, but he hadn't listened. He hadn't wanted to know what could go wrong.

He'd had Dawson call for an appointment with the eye specialist, delaying it until tomorrow. He wanted a full night of hope with Brittany first. Hope that his eyesight would indeed return.

"WOULD YOU LISTEN TO this," Francesca said, munching on a bagel and reading from *People* magazine at breakfast the following morning.

"What?" Brittany looked up expectantly from her bowl of fresh fruit.

"What's-her-name is getting a divorce." Francesca slathered light cream cheese on the rest of her bagel.

"Who's What's-her-name?"

"You know, Ethan's ex-fiancée. The one who jilted him."

"Really?"

"Yes, really. There's a picture and everything."

"But I don't understand. Why is she in *People* magazine? She's not a celebrity or anything."

"No, but her soon-to-be-ex-husband is marrying one. Some actress on one of the soaps."

"Let me see," Brittany said, reaching for the magazine.

"You're right, it is her." Brittany wrinkled her nose. "And she still looks great."

"What are you worried about? You're the one with her old fiancé."

"What if she wants him back?" Brittany said with a sinking feeling.

"I'm sure he doesn't want her. They don't even travel in the same circles anymore. She's in L.A., Ethan's in New York."

"Yeah, you're right," Brittany said, relaxing.

"So how are things going with you and Ethan, anyway?"

"Well, he's asked me to go to his class reunion with him next weekend."

"That's great. It's your birthday and you've got a date with Ethan. You must be thrilled."

"I am." Brittany toyed with her fruit cup. "Unless . . . You don't think *she'd* show up at the reunion, do you?"

"No. Of course not. Probably not."

"But what if she does?"

"Then she does. What are you so worried about? Don't you have an early meeting today?"

"Oh gosh, I almost forgot." Brittany pushed her fruit cup away and stood to collect her things for the office.

"I've got an eleven o'clock flight to the coast today, so don't wait up," Francesca said casually as Brittany checked her watch and picked up her briefcase.

"You got the video!" Brittany screamed, dropping her briefcase and throwing her arms around her sister.

"I got the video!" Francesca screamed right back, as they jumped up and down hugging each other as if they'd just won a tag-team game of jacks.

BRITTANY SAT IN HER office with the door closed.

If her day got any better, she'd faint.

Her assistant had just quit. It seemed the West Coast agent had offered her a job as an agent trainee and Sandy had decided there was more glitz and glamour in L.A.

Now, if only Tricia would stay in L.A. and out of the picture where Ethan was concerned . . .

She cleared her head and concentrated, editing the final chapters of a mystery by a new author she'd acquired.

Right before lunch her assistant brought her another piece of good news. The *USA Today* bestseller list that was published every Thursday listed one of Brittany's romance authors at number thirty-two.

That was a coup, as the list reflected cash-register sales of the top fifty hard/soft, fiction/nonfiction books in the entire country.

After she made a celebratory call to the author and had Sandy send her a bouquet of flowers, Brittany treated herself to lunch at the new Barney's uptown store. She had a sandwich in the Chelsea Café, then taxied back to her building.

Back in her office, Brittany sat down to work on her speeches for the upcoming sales conference. It wasn't to be, however.

There was one flaw in her perfect day and she couldn't avoid it any longer. Tricia What's-her-name was getting a divorce.

She would have to tell Ethan the truth.

It was a risk, she knew. A very big risk.

But she didn't have a choice. If Tricia showed up at the reunion . . . !

WHEN SHE GOT HOME from the office there was a message on her answering machine from Dawson, telling her not to eat dinner.

Ethan had made plans.

Oh, great, she thought, kicking off her shoes and tossing down her briefcase. Dawson hadn't said what the plans were.

Hours later, as they sat listening to jazz at the Blue Note Club in the Village, Brittany was glad she'd decided to dress up.

Ethan Moss knew how to give good date.

Once she'd arrived at his apartment, he'd whisked them off on a fifteen-minute helicopter tour of Manhattan. The weather was perfect and it felt positively decadent to be flying above the rush-hour traffic. She'd never been in a helicopter before and loved the feeling of freedom.

The helicopter pilot returned them to the limo Ethan had hired for the evening and they were off to the Metropolitan Museum of Art, which stayed open later on Friday evenings.

There, as they'd walked through a tiny part of the museum, she had described the exhibits to Ethan. He'd linked his arm with hers and allowed her to lead him. The fact that he was letting the world know they were a couple thrilled her.

Afterward, they'd sat on the mezzanine at a table decorated with little candles and listened to a string quartet. Then, as now, she had rested her head on his shoulder and enjoyed the romance she had been so starved for with the only man who could quench her hunger. She knew she'd had a giddy smile on her face the whole time she'd sat there fiddling with the earrings Ethan had bought her in the museum shop.

From there, the limo driver had taken them to the next place Ethan had mapped out for their date.

Like a freshman taking a junior to the prom, he'd gone all out to impress. He'd made reservations for them at Robert De Niro's Tribeca Grill. She'd loved it.

The restaurant had been glamorous and noisy, like a big party. They'd shared a bottle of wine over dinner.

Brittany hoped the wine would help her summon the nerve to do what she had to do. It was time.

She'd put it off long enough, having allowed herself this one perfect romantic evening with Ethan in case he hated her after she told him what she'd done. In case he never wanted to see her again.

She wouldn't be able to blame him, either.

"I HOPE YOU HAD AS great an evening as I did," Ethan whispered when he forced his lips from hers. They were back on the library sofa. "Did you enjoy yourself tonight?"

"Very much," Brittany assured him.

"Does this mean you're going to read me a bedtime story and stay to tuck me in?"

"As a matter of fact I brought the new issue of *People* magazine. There was something in it I wanted to read to you."

Acting before she could talk herself out of doing what she knew was right, Brittany eased her way out of Ethan's embrace, and got up from the sofa to retrieve the magazine.

"I feel I should tell you I haven't ever felt the need to read *People* magazine," he said. "My mother's daily phone calls keep me up-to-date with more than I want to know about people, especially people I don't even know."

Brittany hadn't thought of that. Hadn't thought someone might already have told him about Tricia's divorce. It was the kind of thing a mother would relay. Particularly Ethan's very social mother.

After locating the magazine, Brittany returned to the sofa to sit beside Ethan. "Okay, now stop me if you've already heard about this," she told him, and began hunting up the page.

She found it and started reading. "'Patrick York, the ace reliever for baseball's California Angels, has announced he is divorcing socialite Tricia Edwards to marry soap star Monica Collins, who plays Jessie on "The Restless Heart." The ex-Mrs. York is relocating to New York.'"

Ethan didn't comment right away. "Mother missed telling me that, somehow," he said finally.

"How do you feel about it?" Brittany probed.

"About what?"

"Tricia—"

"I told you I didn't talk about her," Ethan said, cutting off the questions she would have asked.

But she wasn't to be refused.

"Why?"

"Because Tricia taught me about the deceitfulness of a woman. It took me a long time to find a woman I could really trust after her. I didn't think I ever would until I found you, freckle face." He pulled her toward him, brushing a kiss on her nose. "You've forced me to open my eyes."

"Did you ever forgive her for running off with another man on your wedding day?"

"It's not the sort of thing a man would ever forgive. Or forget," he said softly.

"Ethan?"

"Hmm . . . ?"

"Will you listen to something I have to tell you and not say anything until I've finished?"

"What's this all about?" he asked, picking up the quaver in her voice, her nervousness.

"Will you promise to just listen and hear me out?"

"But—"

"Promise."

"Okay. I'm listening."

"I remember the first time I saw you. I was fourteen years old. You were playing polo. I think I fell in love with you on sight. I don't know how to explain it. Some people might say we were together in another life, that that was why you seemed so right. Or just that it was a young girl's first infatuation."

She moved nervously beside him on the sofa and continued, "Whatever, it didn't go away.

"I turned into your biggest fan, only you didn't know it because I was so much younger than you . . . and I was very shy.

"I filled scrapbooks with news clippings and photos and anything else I could find on you. Francesca teased me constantly about it, about you. I accepted her teasing because I knew that someday when I was old enough, you and I would be together. I just knew it. I believed it."

She took a deep breath to quiet her nerves. "The worst day of my life was when Francesca told me you'd become engaged to Tricia Edwards. I was crushed that you hadn't waited for me. I know that was totally unreasonable, but I couldn't help how I felt."

She couldn't look at him as she finally revealed the secret she'd carried all these years. Guilt washed over her as she blurted, "Poor Francesca got the full brunt of my misery. I was a hopeless case. Finally—I think in a desperate attempt to snap me out of it—she flippantly suggested I try to do something to help myself rather than wallow in my own misery.

"Of course, she'd meant take up tennis or another hobby and fall in love with someone else.

"I took it to mean find a way to make you see that Tricia wasn't the right woman for you. To make you change your mind about marrying her."

Ethan was very still beside her. She got up from the sofa and began pacing.

"So I began planning.

"But I couldn't think of any way to make you change your mind about Tricia. She was so beautiful.

"It wasn't until right before your wedding that I hit upon an idea. I pestered Francesca until she agreed to help me with it."

Brittany paused, glancing over at Ethan, but he said nothing.

She took a deep breath and continued before her nerve left her.

"At the time, Francesca was dating a baseball player, and there was this other player on the team, Patrick York, who was considered a real ladies' man. It was a reputation he took great pleasure in. Francesca used to talk about him because she and her baseball player would often double with Patrick, and he'd have a different girl every time they dated.

"Since I knew you were having a bachelor party with all your polo buddies the night before your wedding, I had Francesca talk Tricia into having a bachelorette party the same night. Then, using all the money I had saved up, I pestered Francesca until she agreed to wager my thousand dollars with Patrick York that he couldn't get Tricia Edwards to fly to Las Vegas with him the night before her wedding."

There was still nothing; no response of any kind from Ethan.

Brittany gave a nervous little laugh.

"Well, of course, it was an offer his ego couldn't refuse.

"And you know the rest."

Her voice took on a pleading tone. "But I couldn't have known that she would *marry* Patrick York in Las Vegas that night and you'd wake up on your wedding day to find the announcement in the headlines."

A tear rolled down her cheek. "I'm sorry, Ethan. I'm so sorry." Her voice quavered. "I know what I did was wrong, but I never meant to hurt you. I just loved you so much...."

Brittany didn't know what to expect—what Ethan's reaction would be when she told him the truth about her part in Tricia's deceit.

For the longest time he didn't react at all. He just sat there. The room was as silent as a crypt.

When he finally spoke, his voice was cold and emotionless. "I'd like you to leave now. I'll have Dawson mail you your check. Leave the key on the hall table."

"But—"

"Just go."

His words were final.

"Ethan, please don't hate me. I couldn't bear it if you hated me," she pleaded.

But he wouldn't answer her.

ETHAN HEARD THE DOOR close as Brittany let herself out. He picked up the *People* magazine she'd left on the sofa and threw it across the room with an oath.

Ethan cursed the female sex, every deceitful one of them. He'd been a fool—not once, but twice.

Anger coursed through him until he shook. It was an icy cold anger that froze his heart. No woman would ever, ever melt his defenses again.

He knew what he was going to do. He was going to the stables in the morning after his appointment with the eye doctor. Maybe he could ride off his anger. At least he knew his horse wouldn't ride under a tree branch and brush him off the way a woman would when you were least expecting it.

His eyesight might be returning, but his judgment concerning women was just as bad as it had always been.

It was time he got back to playing polo as if his life depended on it. He was very much afraid that his sanity certainly did.

It had hurt when Tricia had stood him up at the altar, but her deceit had mostly wounded a young man's pride, his masculine ego.

Brittany's deceit hurt far deeper.

BRITTANY TRIED TO WILL the tears that were welling in her eyes to stop, but they didn't. She felt like a fool sobbing in the back of the taxi, but she couldn't stop.

Ethan had told her he never wanted to see her again. And he'd said it with such quiet fury that she believed him. In an instant, she had destroyed whatever he had felt for her.

He would never forgive her.

BRITTANY TOOK FRIDAY as an at-home reading day. She didn't want to face the questions her red eyes and nose and puffy face would raise.

But before she attempted to plow her way through the stack of manuscripts, she went out to the balcony with her morning coffee and puttered with her roses in their terra-cotta tubs and English ivy in wooden boxes. Her garden did quite well even though it got only a few hours of direct sunlight.

A circulating water fountain massed with climbing hydrangea encouraged the mourning doves—that and the fanciful birdhouses she'd put out.

She had already gone through a box of tissues and was reduced to carrying around a roll of toilet paper with her to stem the sudden bursts of tears.

It hadn't occurred to her that it would hurt worse to lose something you had, than never to have had it at all.

As she clipped the fading roses and put them in a bag for potpourri, she lectured herself. But it didn't do any good—she was heartbroken.

For the first time in her life, she knew what the term meant.

Noon found her curled up asleep in the old ironwood chair on the balcony. She hadn't slept all night and it had finally caught up with her. She woke up with a start when the manuscript on her lap fell with a thud.

She wondered what Ethan was doing . . . thinking. And if he was thinking about her. She glanced at the answering machine to see if maybe he might have reconsidered. If, having slept on it, he had come to realize she hadn't meant to harm him, not really. But there was no blinking green light, no message from Ethan.

No hope.

SATURDAY MORNING SHE was still in bed when "Style" came on, on CNN.

Nothing appealed to her. She couldn't get interested in the clothes, or the jewelry or even the castle one of the European designers had refurbished to make his country home.

Feeling blue, she decided to go out and shop for the cat she'd promised herself.

Maybe having a cat would help her deal with the gloom that had shrouded her in despair when Ethan had ordered her from his life.

She got dressed after her shower, and headed out to try to enjoy the beautiful day. On her way she got distracted at Bloomingdale's where she pampered herself with the new Godiva vanilla-hazelnut coffee; *pampered* was the right word because the stuff cost her ten dollars for ten ounces. Trying to spend herself into a better mood, she bought a set of designer sheets, as well, telling herself their luxurious softness would help her sleep.

Of course her shopping trip reminded her of her visit to Saks with Ethan and she started getting weepy again. She headed to the perfume counter. A new fragrance always promised to restore self-esteem.

She bought into every sentimental perfume ad she'd ever seen. Like a brand-new perfume, Ethan had made her feel beautiful and special. In fact she could have sworn she'd almost felt herself glow.

Now she was glowing because her nose was red.

By the time she was through at Bloomingdale's, guilt had set in. The cat got put on hold. Instead, she went home to her apartment and pulled herself together enough to sift through the manuscripts she'd been avoiding. She even found a real possibility; a new author to champion.

There was nothing like making that first phone call to an unpublished author. It was like being Merlin the Magician for a brief moment, able to make a person's dream become a reality when you relayed the news that the publisher wanted to buy their manuscript.

Of course, there were a lot of steps that had to be gone through before she could actually make that call. For starters, she would have to convince the editorial group that they should buy the book.

But she had a really good feeling about this particular manuscript. It had made her laugh at a time when she couldn't have felt less like laughing.

Finding the book in the slush pile had done something buying the perfume had not. It had restored her self-esteem. It had reminded her that she was good at her job.

If only she were good at forgetting Ethan Moss.

BRITTANY WAS SITTING in the middle of her bed in her socks and T-shirt looking through the ads to see if anyone had a Bengal kitten for sale when the phone rang.

She made a lunge for the phone, answering it on the first ring, her heart leaping with the impossible hope that the caller might be Ethan.

It wasn't.

"Brittany, are you sick? You don't sound so good. What's wrong?" Francesca asked.

"I'm fine. No, that's not true. I'm a wreck. I've been crying a lot. That's why I sound so lousy."

"Ethan didn't take what you had to tell him very well, did he?"

"No."

"Listen, I'm flying in this afternoon. I would have called to check on you earlier, but the video was filmed on this primitive island."

"How did the filming go?"

"Great. As a matter of fact, the director said he might be able to use me on another project he's shooting next month."

"That's wonderful news, Francesca! But what about Tucker? I haven't heard you say anything about him."

"Tucker Gable is a total sweetheart," Francesca said, her voice hinting of hope. "He's flying back to New York with me."

"Oh? Shall I tell Mother when I call her later?"

"No! He's coming on business."

"Uh-huh."

"Goodbye, Brittany."

Brittany sat with the phone in her hand not even hearing the drone of the dial tone.

Her feelings were bittersweet.

She was happy for Francesca. Happy her sister had found Tucker Gable, even if her sister couldn't see what a blind man could see.

A blind man...

She wanted to cry but didn't. She was a grown woman. If her fate was to be a spinster with a cat, she'd face it.

After all she had a great career.

A great...empty life. She started to cry.

11

WHEN BRITTANY ARRIVED at the French Roast, the French café on Sixth Avenue, Francesca and Tucker were already there.

It was a shame Francesca didn't do rock stars, because they looked stunning together. Stunning and right. And whether Francesca knew it or not, she looked like a woman in love.

Brittany made her way across the black-and-white tile floor to the two small tables they'd pushed together to form a table for four—except it was for three.

She was alone.

After introductions, Brittany slid onto a wooden chair across from them.

"So, you're an editor, huh?" Tucker said. "Have you edited anything I might have read lately?"

"Yeah, like rock stars read," Francesca taunted.

"We read, all right. We just like a few pictures to break up the print."

"Pictures of naked women, you mean?"

"What's wrong with naked women? God doesn't make junk, you know."

"You're impossible," Francesca said, shaking her head and catching a waiter's eye.

Brittany and Francesca ordered the French salad plate while Tucker opted for the traditional pot-au-feu.

"Mind if I join you?"

Brittany recognized the voice.

Francesca looked shocked.

Tucker looked puzzled.

Without waiting for an answer, Ethan stepped from behind the waiter and took the chair next to Brittany.

"Nothing for me," Ethan said, waving off the waiter.

Once again, Francesca made introductions.

"Glad to meet you, dude. Sorry to hear about that nasty spill you took. How are you doing?" Tucker asked, genuinely interested.

"My eyesight's returned and my doctor gave me a clean bill of health. I can't complain."

Ethan could see again! Brittany wanted to crawl into a hole. She also wanted to grab him and hug him with joy.

How had he known where to find her? The answer had to be Sandy. Brittany hadn't been able to resist telling her assistant she was meeting Tucker, just to make Sandy pea green with envy.

"So where did you two meet?" Ethan asked Francesca.

"I did a cover for *Rolling Stone* with Tucker. It'll be out in a few months."

Brittany couldn't bring herself to say anything. To even look at Ethan.

Why was he here?

She couldn't allow herself to hope that he'd changed his mind about her. That he'd realized she'd told him the truth because she loved him. That he'd remembered she was a love-starved, foolish teenager when she pulled the stunt.

"What are you up to, Ethan? I haven't seen much of you in the columns lately," Francesca asked.

"I haven't been social since the accident. But I'm planning to remedy that. As a matter of fact, that's why I'm here. I wanted to ask Brittany to attend my class reunion with me."

He had turned to look at her.

"What do you say, Brittany?"

"I, ah..." she stammered, amazed he would ask her.

The waiter came with their entrées, and she had a momentary reprieve.

"It seems my ex-fiancée is going to be at the reunion and she's been recently divorced."

"Oh, I get it. You want to make her squirm so you're asking a pretty girl like Brittany to decorate your arm," Tucker said, endearing himself to Brittany forever.

"Something like that," Ethan said, not taking his eyes off her. "So, what do you say? Will you go with me?"

Francesca and Tucker pretended to be terribly occupied with their food.

Brittany knew exactly what he was saying. She could read it in his eyes. She owed him, because of what she'd done. He was putting her on the spot, asking her to do something she'd already agreed to under very different circumstances.

Tucker had it all wrong.

Ethan wasn't taking her to show her off. He was taking her to make her pay for what she'd done. He planned to get Tricia back.

And he planned to make her watch.

There was no way she could do that.

"Aw, come on, woman. Put him out of his misery and say yes," Tucker urged.

She supposed she had to. It was that or make a scene. And she did owe him.

"Yes," she said softly, reluctantly.

"Okay. Then it's a date. I'll pick you up on Saturday at eight," Ethan said, with a glint of victory in his eyes.

The waiter returned to the table with their drink order and Ethan took the opportunity to excuse himself.

"But before I leave, I wonder if I could speak with you alone for a moment, Tucker."

Brittany was already half out of her chair and sat back down as unobtrusively as possible when Ethan said Tucker's name instead of hers.

"Sure, man," Tucker replied, rising to go out to the sidewalk with Ethan.

"What do you suppose they're talking about?" Brittany asked.

"Who knows?" Francesca said, shrugging. "They're probably comparing tattoos."

Brittany began to cry.

"Oh, honey, don't do that. He asked you out. Everything is going to be okay."

"No, it's not. He only asked me to punish me. He wants Tricia back, not me."

"What makes you think that?"

"I ruined his life when I stopped his wedding."

"He was angry. Maybe he reconsidered."

"No. He hates me."

"Who hates you?" Tucker asked, rejoining them.

"The waiter."

"Why?"

"Never mind. What were you and Ethan talking about out there?"

Tucker laughed. "Nothing. The guy's a crazy man."

"What?"

"Never mind, let's eat. I'm starved. Then after we eat maybe we can take in a movie or something."

"*The Age of Innocence?*" Brittany and Francesca both said hopefully.

"Or maybe we could go to the Village and listen to some jazz."

Brittany started to cry again.

"What'd I say?" Tucker asked, looking mortified.

"Nothing. Eat your pot-au-feu."

Tucker picked at his plate with his fork. "But it's boiled carrots and cabbage and lots of vegetables."

"So why did you order it, if you don't like vegetables?" Francesca asked.

"The only other choice was the salad you guys got or calf's liver—yuck."

He signaled the waiter, who came immediately to their table.

"Do you have desserts?"

The waiter rattled off a sweet-and-tangy tart, a crème caramel and a chocolate-iced opera cake.

"One of each and we'll all sample," Tucker ordered.

After dessert Tucker lived up to Francesca's "total sweetheart" billing and took them to a late showing of *The Age of Innocence*.

It gave Brittany a chance to have a good cry.

Francesca a chance to rave over the dresses.

And Tucker a chance to say that there was no reason to ever marry, save love.

Which endeared him to both women forever.

Tucker Gable was an endearing sort of guy.

Too bad Ethan Moss wasn't, Brittany thought with a sniff, wondering how she was ever going to get through Saturday night.

12

BRITTANY ASTOR HAD decided she wasn't going down without a fight.

Still, she wasn't quite sure about the red sheath she'd bought. From the front it showed off her curves but nothing more. It was the back that was scandalous.

There *wasn't* one. It was scooped down to there.

"You look fabulous. Will you quit worrying?" Francesca said, applying the matching red lipstick to Brittany's lips with the expertise she'd learned from watching countless makeup artists do her.

"Ethan probably won't notice. I might as well be wearing a gunnysack. He'll only have eyes for Tricia Edwards. I don't stand a chance against her. I *never* did."

"You aren't a kid anymore, baby sister. Look in the mirror."

Her reflection showed Francesca was telling the truth. Brittany hardly recognized the woman staring back at her. Francesca had skillfully covered the dusting of freckles on her nose and styled her hair in a sophisticated French twist.

"Wait till you see the shoes I have . . ." Francesca said, heading for her closet.

The telephone rang.

Maybe it was Ethan canceling, Brittany thought with both hope and disappointment.

It was Dawson, telling her Ethan had been detained and would be sending a taxi to pick her up.

Just like old times, she thought, putting down the phone. And she was just as nervous as she'd been the first time Ethan had sent a taxi for her.

Francesca returned from the depths of her closet with a pair of killer pumps: red grosgrain against matte-gold three-inch heels.

"Who was that?"

"Dawson. Ethan's running late, so he's sending a taxi."

"I was hoping maybe it was Tucker."

"What is this?" Brittany asked, taking the heels from her sister and slipping into them. "Don't tell me you're smitten, big sister. Sitting around at home waiting for a man to call you?"

"He's just so much fun. And he isn't stuck on himself. And he really, really likes women. I mean, likes them as people. Enjoys them. That's so refreshing after all the macho, self-absorbed, jock-mentality guys I've dated."

"Okay, so you don't like him," Brittany said with a laugh. "What's he doing in New York, anyway? Did he come just to be with you?"

"No. He's here talking to some galleries about his paintings."

"Ah, a Renaissance man," Brittany said, slipping on the diamond ear studs she'd gotten to wear for her debut.

"He is, sort of. You have to give him a lot of credit, coming from the abused childhood he ran away from. He could have turned to drugs and crime."

"Oh, so we've progressed to talking about childhoods. Sounds pretty serious to me, big sister. Are you sure I shouldn't call Mom and tell her a grandbaby might not be such a farfetched idea? That she ought to be buying *Bride's* magazine instead of the fashion magazines to look for your pictures?"

"We're just pals," Francesca assured her, somewhat wistfully.

"So then you haven't kissed or anything."

"Well, I wouldn't go that far."

"Is he a good kisser?"

"Is Grisham on the *New York Times* list? What do you think? Ah, your taxi is here," Francesca said, handing Brittany her Fendi bag. "You look stunning. Now go knock 'em dead."

"What are you going to do tonight?"

"Sit around and watch an old movie on television, I guess."

"You mean sit around and wait for the phone to ring," Brittany teased.

"Go," Francesca ordered.

SHE HAD EXPECTED Dawson to open the door.

But it was Ethan who stood before her, not quite dressed. He had on gray suit pants and was shrugging into his shirt. It was unbuttoned, revealing his smooth, muscled chest and washboard belly.

He was playing very dirty.

"Come on in," he said, spider to fly.

"What time is the reunion? Aren't we going to be late?" she asked, flustered, as she followed him into the library.

"It's fashionable to be late. Wait here and I'll be ready shortly." He was playing really dirty, leaving her with a room full of memories.

They were fashionably late.

And greatly anticipated. Well, Ethan was, if the titter that rippled through the crowd at their arrival was any indication.

"Over here, Ethan," a short boisterous man called out from one of the round white-linen-covered tables near the dais.

Ethan led her to the table, his hand at her back as if she might bolt, given the chance. And he wasn't half wrong. It was her strongest urge, next to her urge to throw up.

She'd spotted Tricia Edwards at the table where they were to sit.

Ethan held her chair while he made introductions. The short boisterous man was successful in the garment district. His wife, Bunny, had a dinner ring on each finger. Another polo player with his date, a model, and Tricia Edwards, who was there alone, made up the table.

The salad had already been served and Brittany played with hers while someone on the dais read off a list of awards for everything from Most Children to Biggest Surprise.

The one for Biggest Surprise went to the cheerleader who had gone on to edit a feminist magazine. Brittany thought her being there with Ethan would have won if Tricia could have voted—she hadn't taken her eyes off Ethan since they'd arrived.

Brittany hoped they'd be very happy together.

No, she didn't. That was a lie.

The table was cleared of the salads and the waiter brought the entrée while classmates came and went from the table, all with the same message: They'd known Ethan would see again, that he would be fine. The implication being that if he hadn't regained his sight, he would have been socially undesirable.

Just before dessert, the last speaker finished and the class president took the microphone. "Now it's time for everyone to enjoy themselves, and we'll start it off with the first dance of the evening. It's been suggested to me that the first dance be begun by the King and Queen of the Sweetheart Dance."

Brittany got a sinking feeling in the pit of her stomach. She glanced over to see Tricia begin scooting back her chair. The smug smile on her face told just who had suggested the idea. Brittany didn't have to look to her side to know that Ethan had been king to Tricia's queen.

A sudden inspiration hit Brittany. When Ethan got up and danced with Tricia, she could sneak out. She would have honored his request. She'd gone to the reunion with him. And she'd been properly humiliated. He could leave with Tricia.

Ethan would have paid her back for her prank all those years ago, and she would have delivered Tricia back to him.

Brittany heard Ethan whisper something to the polo player as Tricia came around the table and placed her hand in Ethan's. Looking frail and beautiful, Tricia clung to Ethan as he led her out onto the dance floor.

A perfect vision, the couple circled the floor a few times and then the class president announced that everyone was to join them.

Brittany breathed a sigh of relief; it was her cue to bolt. If she could manage it without the tears she was trying to hold at bay, all the better.

She reached for her purse, only to have the polo player cover her hand with his. "Uh-uh... No trip to the ladies' room now. This dance was promised to me."

"But I didn't..." Brittany started to object.

"I know. Ethan did," he explained, insisting she join him on the dance floor.

So that was what Ethan had whispered. He was making sure she stayed to witness his reunion with Tricia.

It was strange, she thought, as she danced with the man and felt her gaze drawn to the back of Ethan's head and Tricia's beaming look of conquest—tonight she wasn't envious of Tricia's beauty.

Brittany realized that she was comfortable with who she was. That not having based her self-esteem on something as frivolous as looks, she'd developed into someone she quite liked, even if Ethan didn't.

She might not be beautiful, but she was attractive.

Beauty wasn't the issue. Ethan was.

It was just her bad luck he preferred beautiful women.

Tricia and Ethan were dancing closer together and Brittany thought she might cry if he looked at her in pity. She had to get off the dance floor. Had to get out of the stifling ballroom. Her prayers were answered when her partner slowed his steps.

"Excuse me a moment," he said, leaving her.

She turned away, not seeing him go to cut in on Ethan and Tricia.

Deciding this was her chance to escape, Brittany grabbed her purse and made a beeline for the exit.

"Brittany."

She didn't turn around. It was only her too-fertile imagination making her think she was hearing Ethan calling out her name.

"Brittany, wait."

Really, she admonished herself, she had to start accepting what was, not dreaming of what could never be.

"Damn it, Brittany, wait."

The curse stopped her dead in her tracks. Either she was hopelessly romantic or Ethan was distressed that she was leaving.

He caught up to her.

"What are you doing?" he demanded.

"Making it easy for you."

"By leaving?"

"I thought I'd give you a clear shot at Tricia."

"We need to talk. But first . . ."

He pulled her into his arms and she stared at him incredulously.

"Don't look at me like you don't know what you look like in that dress."

An ache rose in her throat. Why was he toying with her like this? Had she hurt him that badly? Of course, she had.

She looked into his eyes and her mind went completely blank as his lips claimed hers. It wasn't a sweet kiss; it was a claiming kiss.

Confusion warred with passion as the kiss deepened, lengthened. What was he doing? Why was he doing it? And why couldn't she seem to stop him?

She was trembling when he released her.

"Can—can I go now?" she stuttered, trying to save face while knowing she'd given everything away with her response to his kiss.

"Yes. Let's go."

She thought he was taking her home. Instead, he took her to his brownstone.

Once inside, he pulled her into his arms again.

"I've had a lot of time to think," he explained. "To cool down. To miss you. To realize you were the one who loved me when I wasn't perfect. I can't seem to keep my hands off you. I kept listening for your step, your laugh.

"God, Brittany, I've been miserable without you."

"You have?"

"I've had a lot of time to think this past week," he said, pulling her into the library. I might have been blinded by the accident, but I've been blind for a long time to my needs. All my constant activity was a cover for my loneliness. You opened my eyes, Brittany. When I was sightless, you opened my eyes."

"Are you telling me that you forgive me for what I did?" she asked, holding her breath.

"Yes. It took courage to tell me. You didn't have to. I've let go of my anger, Brittany. I see now that you did what you did because you loved me. I would have made a terrible mistake marrying Tricia."

"But then why did you want to go to the reunion?" she asked, still hurting.

"I wanted to show you off. I wanted to show Tricia how beautiful you are. I should have gotten the award tonight for Luckiest Guy in the Class. Oh Brittany, can you forgive me for how horrible I've been to you?"

She pushed off his jacket and unbuttoned his shirt. "I don't know," she teased. "I might need a little coaxing."

He laughed. "I'm one step ahead of you. Stay right here."

Ethan left the room and Brittany rubbed her temples. Everything was happening so fast. She'd been prepared for . . . she didn't know what, exactly, but it wasn't this.

Ethan could see. And he still wanted her. She hugged that thought to herself.

Could it really be true?

"Ouch!"

"Meow . . ."

Brittany spun around to see a large tabby cat leap from Ethan's arms and run toward her. The cat jumped up on the sofa.

"Aw . . . Where did you come from?" Brittany said, moving to the sofa and sitting down beside the cat to pet it. The animal purred and rubbed up against Brittany.

"His name is Charley. Dawson tells me he's a Maine coon breed that strayed into the stable a week ago. No one has turned up to claim him. According to Dawson, Maine coons are one-person cats. Looks like you're the person," he announced as the cat curled up in Brittany's lap and began a happy purring. "He's grouchy every time I try to hold him."

"He's beautiful," Brittany said in a hushed tone, admiring the cat's double coat and beautiful green eyes set off by its dramatic ear furnishings.

"He's yours."

"Really?"

"Francesca told me you wanted a cat, so I—"

"You've talked to Francesca!"

"Now, don't get mad at her. I made her promise not to tell you. I wanted tonight to be a surprise. I didn't know if you would forgive me for being such a jerk."

"What do you think, Charley, should we forgive him?"

The cat meowed contentedly.

"We forgive you," Brittany assured him.

"Then I only have one other question."

"What's that?"

"Do you like the collar I picked out for Charley?"

"The collar?" she asked, puzzled.

Ethan nodded.

Brittany lifted the cat and the light caught the diamond solitaire engagement ring dangling from Charley's leather collar.

"Ethan!"

"Is that a yes?" he asked, hopefully.

Brittany dropped Charley to the sofa and leapt up to drape her arms around Ethan's neck.

"Ask me nicely..." she teased.

"Will you marry me, Brittany? Please...?"

She pretended to be considering his offer. "Ask me not-so-nicely—"

He crushed her lips in a deep kiss, his tongue like rough velvet.

"Yes," she moaned moments later when she could breathe again.

"I love you, freckle face."

"Will you stop calling me that? Oh, I've got to call Francesca. Wait till she hears!" Brittany couldn't hide her excitement.

She went to the phone and punched in the number and waited.

There was no answer.

"She must have fallen asleep," Brittany said, disappointed.

"You can tell her in the morning."

"*Morning?*"

"Well, it may take us till morning to find Charley, so I can put my ring on your finger," Ethan said, looking around for the cat, who had disappeared.

"Here kitty, kitty..."

They found him hiding in the kitchen, and Ethan slipped the engagement ring on Brittany's finger.

"What are you thinking?" Ethan asked.

"I was thinking this has been a perfect ending to what I'd anticipated would be the worst night of my life."

"Ending? But the night is still young. Do you realize we haven't made love since my sight has returned?" Ethan's voice was husky with desire.

She'd forgotten he'd never seen her naked. All her insecurities came flooding back, despite the red dress that made her feel so sexy.

"And I thought," she heard him saying, "turnabout would only be fair."

"What are you talking about?" She watched him slowly loosen his tie.

"Come along and I'll show you," he said, taking her hand and leading her upstairs to the bedroom.

"Close your eyes," he instructed.

She found herself doing as she was told, because when she closed her eyes her fears seemed to vanish. He looped his tie around her head, covering her eyes, effectively blindfolding her.

She heard him opening and closing drawers.

"What are you doing?"

"Looking for more ties. Hadn't you noticed the iron bed has four posters, after a fashion—"

"Ethan...!"

"Okay, so I'll only get *two* more ties...."

She'd never be able to wear the red dress again.

Ethan was a novice at this game he'd fancied, because once he'd located the ties and had her squirming with mock protest on the bed, there was only one way to get her out of the red dress.

And then he wrapped her in the dark velvet that was his voice. He used his mouth on her until he had her sighing with pleasure.

"This isn't fair, you know," she moaned when she wriggled her hips against him, wanting him.

He looked down at her, his eyes heavy and sultry, his grin wicked. "I know."

Every nerve ending in her body sizzled. The fiery ache in her belly had complete control of her—as did Ethan.

She licked his jaw when he lowered his head to kiss her neck. His skin was slick and salty, the line of his jaw hard and firm.

Moving her hips again against the satiny steel of him, she was reckless with hunger.

"You deserve this, you know," he told her when she moaned in frustration, her head twisting from side to side.

"Then give it to me," she practically screamed through clenched teeth.

The laugh that tore from his throat was loud and rich. "Not so hasty, my sweet. Haven't you heard good things come to those who wait?"

"Then you had better be freaking great!"

"Sweetness!" Ethan pretended shock. He grinned at her. "I meant you deserve to be needy for me the way you made me needy for you with your stories—your sexy, outrageous stories."

Brittany arched her body provocatively.

"That isn't fair, sweetness." He frowned, a playful frown. "That isn't fair."

"I know."

"So let's really let down our hair, shall we?" he teased, undoing hers that was already half-undone anyway.

And then his lovemaking began in earnest. And they were exquisite together—their lovemaking first slow and teasing, then hard and passionate.

He'd tied her up and set her free.

IN THE MORNING SHE returned the favor.

And then she fixed them breakfast while trying to call Francesca to tell her her exciting news.

There was no answer.

Francesca must have gone out shopping, Brittany decided, as Ethan pointed out it was past noon and what they were eating was lunch. Charley was, too, with a saucer of milk on the side.

Over their omelets they settled into a comfortable companionship as Ethan told her what it had been like when his eyesight returned. How he'd spent the week drinking in the sight of everything with a newfound appreciation. He told her of his plans to put on a Broadway play and donate the profits to the Lighthouse. He'd been so very lucky and wanted to also see if he couldn't find a way to stage a Broadway play using sightless performers.

There was a polo match on cable, so they adjourned to the library to watch it.

Brittany wore Ethan's pajama top and he wore the bottoms. She lay stretched out on the sofa with her head in his lap, sifting through the Sunday edition of the *New York Times*.

She was looking at the *Book Review* section when a station break made her look up.

The announcer had said something about Chelsea Stone and Tucker Gable—

"Congratulations are in order for country music's hottest duo, Chelsea Stone and Dakota Law. The Laws are proud parents of a son, Tucker Cody Law, born last night at 11:05. The godfather, Tucker Gable, was busy himself last night. Seems he and supermodel Francesca Astor were married in Las Vegas."

Ethan's laughter was deep and rich, at Brittany's yelp of excitement.

Hearing it, she turned to look at him as a guilty flush spread over his face.

"Wait a minute. Why is it that you don't seem surprised?" Brittany demanded.

"Me?" He feigned innocence badly.

"You. Come on, give. What did you do? What did you and Tucker talk about outside the restaurant Monday night?"

"Oh, nothing. I just happened to mention to Tucker that I had known Francesca for a long time. And that I hoped his intentions were honorable. I wasn't too threatening. I think I did mention something about me and my polo cronies. And I dropped a major hint that Francesca had always had this fantasy of a man who would sweep her off her feet and take her to Las Vegas and marry her on the spot."

"Ethan!"

"Well, it serves the two of you right. Kinda brings things full circle, don't you think? Besides . . ."

"Besides what?"

"Besides, you told me you liked stories with happy endings."

"Think you're pretty smooth, don't you? Well, think about this. You know what Francesca eloping means? It means my mother is going to insist we have a big, fancy, blowout wedding."

"My mother wouldn't have it any other way," Ethan countered. After planting a satisfied kiss on her lips he added, "And neither would I."

ETHAN WAS A MAN full of surprises.

After the polo match on television was over, he whisked her off to his stable where her birthday present snorted impatiently in his stall.

She'd finally gotten a pony for her birthday at the ripe old age of twenty-five.

Epilogue

IT WAS TWO IN THE morning.

The waiting room of the maternity ward of New York's finest hospital held only two occupants save the nurse at the desk watching them with interest.

One man was dressed in a very expensive suit, the kind developed on London's Savile Row in the thirties. He was as elegant as Fred Astaire, except his tie was loosened. His only jewelry was a leather-strapped watch and a wedding band.

The other man wore black jeans and a black leather vest. His hair was back in a ponytail, revealing an ear stud. He had on dark glasses and a wedding band.

Both men were pacing the waiting room while waiting to join their wives. Brothers-in-law, they'd been trading war stories while they waited.

"What time is it now?" Tucker asked, after looking at his bare wrist.

"Past two," Ethan answered, glancing at the watch Brittany had given him for his birthday.

"How long have you been here?" Ethan asked.

Tucker shrugged. "Beats me. Forever, I think." He went to the water cooler for something to do.

"You nervous?" Ethan asked.

"No. You?"

"Yeah."

"Me, too."

Ethan laughed. "You ought to think about wearing a watch."

"So Francesca keeps telling me. But then what would I use as an excuse for being late?"

"Diamonds. I find diamonds work really well," Ethan said with a grin.

"I don't know about Brittany, but her sister has been more into pizza and ice cream of late. Especially about this time of the morning."

"Would you believe I'm the one with the cravings for Mexican food?"

"Really?"

"It's true. At least I didn't get morning sickness."

"How did it go in there with Francesca? Did she tell you she was going to put out a contract on your life, like Brittany did me?"

"Yeah, I think seeing me dead about now is the only thing that would please her. How do they stand the pain?"

"I don't know. That's why I came out here. I was feeling faint."

"Me, too."

Ethan eyed the box of cigars Tucker was carrying around under his arm like a football. "I see you came all prepared."

"Yeah, but you might want to rethink that," Tucker said, looking at the videocam Ethan held. "I brought the idea of filming the birth up casuallike, and Francesca said no way."

"I don't think anything is going to make them happy until they have their shapes back. Have you been going through the 'This makes me look fat' shopping trips?"

"For a while. Finally Francesca stole all my shirts."

"That's where mine went—"

"Man, we aren't going to have a chance against them, you know. I couldn't believe it when the ultrasound tests said they were both having girls."

"Yeah, isn't it great?"

"How'd the two of us get so lucky?"

"I don't know. They planned this, you know. We should have known when they made us have a double wedding. And you thought you were going to get off easy by eloping, pal."

"That reminds me. Francesca told me the other night it was never her dream to run off to Las Vegas and get married, though she went willingly enough at the time. What's the deal?"

"Maybe after this is all over, we'll meet for a beer and I'll tell you the whole story."

"Deal."

"Uh, gentlemen," the nurse at the desk called out, motioning them over. "You're wanted inside."

The two men exchanged nervous glances and went off to become real men.

HARLEQUIN®
Temptation

COMING NEXT MONTH

1994 MISTLETOE MARRIAGES
HISTORICAL CHRISTMAS STORIES

With a twinkle of lights and a flurry of snowflakes, Harlequin Historicals presents *Mistletoe Marriages*, a collection of four of the most magical stories by your favorite historical authors. The perfect way to celebrate the season!

Brimming with romance and good cheer, these heartwarming stories will be available in November wherever Harlequin books are sold.

RENDEZVOUS by Elaine Barbieri
THE WOLF AND THE LAMB by Kathleen Eagle
CHRISTMAS IN THE VALLEY by Margaret Moore
KEEPING CHRISTMAS by Patricia Gardner Evans

Add a touch of romance to your holiday with *Mistletoe Marriages* Christmas Stories!

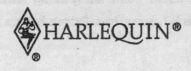

HARLEQUIN®

Where do you find hot Texas nights, smooth Texas charm and dangerously sexy cowboys?

Crystal Creek reverberates with the exciting rhythm of Texas. Each story features the rugged individuals who live and love in the Lone Star state.

"...Crystal Creek wonderfully evokes the hot days and steamy nights of a small Texas community...impossible to put down until the last page is turned."
—*Romantic Times*

"With each book the characters in Crystal Creek become more endearingly familiar. This series is far from formula and a welcome addition to the category genre."
—*Affaire de Coeur*

"Altogether, it couldn't be better."
—*Rendezvous*

Don't miss the next book in this exciting series. Look for
THE HEART WON'T LIE by MARGOT DALTON

Available in January wherever Harlequin books are sold.

CC-23

"HOORAY FOR HOLLYWOOD" SWEEPSTAKES

HERE'S HOW THE SWEEPSTAKES WORKS

OFFICIAL RULES — NO PURCHASE NECESSARY

To enter, complete an Official Entry Form or hand print on a 3" x 5" card the words "HOORAY FOR HOLLYWOOD", your name and address and mail your entry in the pre-addressed envelope (if provided) or to: "Hooray for Hollywood" Sweepstakes, P.O. Box 9076, Buffalo, NY 14269-9076 or "Hooray for Hollywood" Sweepstakes, P.O. Box 637, Fort Erie, Ontario L2A 5X3. Entries must be sent via First Class Mail and be received no later than 12/31/94. No liability is assumed for lost, late or misdirected mail.

Winners will be selected in random drawings to be conducted no later than January 31, 1995 from all eligible entries received.

Grand Prize: A 7-day/6-night trip for 2 to Los Angeles, CA including round trip air transportation from commercial airport nearest winner's residence, accommodations at the Regent Beverly Wilshire Hotel, free rental car, and $1,000 spending money. (Approximate prize value which will vary dependent upon winner's residence: $5,400.00 U.S.); 500 Second Prizes: A pair of "Hollywood Star" sunglasses (prize value: $9.95 U.S. each). Winner selection is under the supervision of D.L. Blair, Inc., an independent judging organization, whose decisions are final. Grand Prize travelers must sign and return a release of liability prior to traveling. Trip must be taken by 2/1/96 and is subject to airline schedules and accommodations availability.

Sweepstakes offer is open to residents of the U.S. (except Puerto Rico) and Canada who are 18 years of age or older, except employees and immediate family members of Harlequin Enterprises, Ltd., its affiliates, subsidiaries, and all agencies, entities or persons connected with the use, marketing or conduct of this sweepstakes. All federal, state, provincial, municipal and local laws apply. Offer void wherever prohibited by law. Taxes and/or duties are the sole responsibility of the winners. Any litigation within the province of Quebec respecting the conduct and awarding of prizes may be submitted to the Regie des loteries et courses du Quebec. All prizes will be awarded; winners will be notified by mail. No substitution of prizes are permitted. Odds of winning are dependent upon the number of eligible entries received.

Potential grand prize winner must sign and return an Affidavit of Eligibility within 30 days of notification. In the event of non-compliance within this time period, prize may be awarded to an alternate winner. Prize notification returned as undeliverable may result in the awarding of prize to an alternate winner. By acceptance of their prize, winners consent to use of their names, photographs, or likenesses for purpose of advertising, trade and promotion on behalf of Harlequin Enterprises, Ltd., without further compensation unless prohibited by law. A Canadian winner must correctly answer an arithmetical skill-testing question in order to be awarded the prize.

For a list of winners (available after 2/28/95), send a separate stamped, self-addressed envelope to: Hooray for Hollywood Sweepstakes 3252 Winners, P.O. Box 4200, Blair, NE 68009.

CBSRLS

OFFICIAL ENTRY COUPON

"Hooray for Hollywood"
SWEEPSTAKES!

Yes, I'd love to win the Grand Prize — a vacation in Hollywood —
or one of 500 pairs of "sunglasses of the stars"! Please enter me
in the sweepstakes!

This entry must be received by December 31, 1994.
Winners will be notified by January 31, 1995.

Name _____

Address _____ Apt. _____

City _____

State/Prov. _____ Zip/Postal Code _____

Daytime phone number _____
(area code)

Account # _____

Return entries with invoice in envelope provided. Each book
in this shipment has two entry coupons — and the more
coupons you enter, the better your chances of winning!

DIRCBS